D1643351

THE GUN MASTER

On his way to visit an old friend, Rex Carey arrives in the township of Willow Creek. But, unbeknownst to him, the infamous Zane Black is staying in the same hotel. Soon Rex, known throughout the West as the Gun Master, clashes with Zane, and blood is spilled. Meanwhile, Forrest Black is riding towards Willow Creek with his men, with no idea he is about to find his brother Zane dead. Determined to avenge him, Forrest and his outlaw gang are on a collision course with Rex . . .

RORY BLACK

---------------------◆---------------------

THE GUN MASTER

Complete and Unabridged

LINFORD
Leicester

First published in Great Britain in 2015 by
Robert Hale Limited
London

First Linford Edition
published 2017
by arrangement with
Robert Hale
an imprint of
The Crowood Press
Wiltshire

A catalogue record for this book is available
from the British Library.

ISBN 978–1–4448–3111–5

Published by
F. A. Thorpe (Publishing)
Anstey, Leicestershire

Set by Words & Graphics Ltd.
Anstey, Leicestershire
Printed and bound in Great Britain by
T. J. International Ltd., Padstow, Cornwall

This book is printed on acid-free paper

Dedicated to my friend Phil Wall

Prologue

Yuma was a town that came to life as soon as the sun set. Its population was nocturnal and lived for the moment. Yesterday was gone and tomorrow might never happen. That was the vague philosophy which seemed to have spread like a cancer throughout all of the people who dwelled within its boundaries. Yet, unlike most other towns, Yuma was suffocated by the smoke stacks of the constant locomotive traffic which constantly rolled in all directions. The choking cloud of black fog never seemed to disperse; it hung over Yuma constantly. Folks tend to get thirsty when there is smoke in the air and that was probably why Yuma boasted more than twenty saloons.

The amber illumination of coal-tar lanterns and lamplight also spread through the vast rail-head. The streets were filled with wagons and riders even at the height of night. They moved between the various stores and businesses as men and women sought and found what they were looking for.

It was said that if you could not find the thing you desired in Yuma then you could not find it anywhere.

Nobody appeared to notice the strange figure that walked down the main street toward the telegraph office. He blended in perfectly with all of the other equally odd creatures that roamed the town that never seemed to sleep. In Yuma he was just another man with his arsenal of weaponry attached to his tall frame. He was just another man who was either a killer or liked to pretend that he was.

But Forrest Black was no pretender.

He was exactly what he appeared to be, a killer that had yet to be discovered and made to pay for his numerous crimes and atrocities. For years, he and the rest of his clan had hired their deadly skills to anyone who could afford them.

Black and his brother Zane were all that remained of their once large family. All of the others had perished as they plied their unwholesome trade. Forrest and Zane Black knew that their days were probably numbered but, as with all men addicted to killing, they continued.

The tall, emaciated figure moved between the riders and hopped up on to the boardwalk outside the telegraph office. He turned the door handle and entered.

Even though the lethal siblings were miles apart, they kept in touch with one another. Zane had always been the brains of the family whilst Forrest had followed his brother's plans and executed them.

Black moved to the desk and looked down at the operator.

'Any messages for me?' Black asked as he bit the end off a cigar and chewed on the six-inch-long remainder.

The small clerk glanced up from his desk. 'Yes indeed, Mr Black. Your brother has sent you a wire. It only came in thirty minutes back.'

Forrest Black snapped his fingers and snatched the small sheet of paper. He pushed his black Stetson up and read the message. He began to nod.

The small man rested his elbows on the desk and looked at Black thoughtfully.

'What does he mean by 'bank job', Mr Black?' he asked.

Forrest Black folded the paper up and slid it into his vest pocket. His narrowed eyes moved to the curious telegraph operator.

'Why do you ask?'

'I was just wondering.' The man shrugged. 'Sounds like your brother wants to get you into trouble.'

Black ran a match along his pants leg, raised it to his cigar and inhaled the strong smoke. He shook the match and tossed it over his shoulder as he continued to stare down at the small man.

'Who else has read this wire?' Black casually asked.

The man shrugged again. 'Only me. Like I said it only came in about thirty minutes back. Why do you ask?'

Without uttering another word, Forrest Black turned to the door and pulled its blind down. He then slid the bolt and secured the door.

'What are you doing, Mr Black?' the clerk asked, becoming alarmed. 'We ain't closed. We never close.'

Black swung on his heels and faced the man. He sucked in smoke and lifted the desk flap and moved toward the trembling man.

'You know what my brother meant, don't you?' Black said through a cloud of cigar smoke as he advanced toward the cornered clerk.

'Sure I do,' the man said as he stepped backward until his retreat was blocked by his chair. 'I ain't stupid. He's told you to come to Willow Creek because he has a bank job planned.'

Forrest Black shook his head.

'You can see my problem, can't you?' he said. 'You've figured out what Zane meant. That ain't healthy for a little man like you to have that kinda knowledge.'

The telegraph operator could see the evil in Black's eyes as he loomed over him.

'I'd never tell anyone,' he said, fearfully. 'Honest, Mr Black. I'd never tell anyone about that wire.'

Black laughed. It was the laughter only a maniac could create. His powerful hands grabbed the clerk and pushed him into the wall.

'Zane taught me a long time ago that witnesses can get you hanged,' Black said as the fingers of his left hand gripped the clerk's throat. He began to squeeze as the frail figure's eyes bulged. 'Nothing personal but rules are rules. You know enough to hang me and Zane, and I can't allow that.'

Forrest Black kept throttling the far smaller man until every ounce of life was mangled from him. He released his grip and the man slumped to the floor.

Black pulled the cigar from his lips

and tapped the ash on to what was left of the telegraph operator. He then blew the lamplight out and turned back toward the door.

As he puffed on his cigar his twisted mind told him what he had to do next. He nodded as he listened to the voices that filled his rancid brain.

'I gotta round up four gunmen and then ride to Willow Creek,' he muttered. 'Then, when we get there, Zane will tell us what to do next. That's it.'

Black slid the bolt across. Before he left the office he looked back at his handiwork. He smiled and puffed hard on his cigar.

'*Adios*,' he said before leaving the telegraph office and blending in with all the other strange creatures who roamed the streets of Yuma.

1

Willow Creek was tranquil. The last of
the town's saloons, gambling halls and
whorehouses had finally closed for what
was left of the dark, moonless night. One
by one the street lights had been extin-
guished until the only light to break through
the black shadows was the glowing coals
of the livery at the very edge of the remote
settlement. It seemed as if every living soul
within the boundaries of Willow Creek
was in bed catching a few fleeting moments
of shut-eye before the sun rose once again.

It was roughly three in the morning
when the silence was broken by the
sound of the horse's hoofs as they
moved between the rambling structures
before riding into Front Street.

The high-shouldered animal was strut-
ting as all stallions with sap in their
branches tend to do as its rider sat astride
its wide girth. The grey nervously eyed

every dark recess and shadow as it was silently steered down the centre of the long, wide street.

The scent of a hundred or more chimney stacks filled the rider's flared nostrils as he allowed his mount to continue its long walk deeper into the town. Just like the grey, his eyes moved from one shadow to the next in search of the gun he knew would one day have the guts to be aimed at him.

Darkness was both his enemy and his friend.

For more than fifteen years he had used the shadow of night as a shield. Never once in all that time had he ever ridden into a strange town until the sun had set and most of its illumination had been snuffed out. Yet he was not a coward as some might have imagined — just a man who was cautious.

In his line of work it paid to be cautious.

His long, slim fingers teased the reins to his left and encouraged the grey toward the tall, weathered livery stable.

The glowing of its forge and the coals within its stout belly cascaded across the dark street and danced on the silver livery of the stallion as Rex Carey eased back and stopped the handsome animal.

The horseman glanced around his wide shoulders until he was sure that his arrival had not been seen or heard by any of the townsfolk. Only then did Carey swing his long right leg over the cantle of his saddle.

He stood holding his reins in his left hand as his right hand rested upon the grip of his holstered .45. He stood just shy of six feet two inches and was as trim as most men could only wistfully dream about being. Every sinew of Carey was honed like a straight razor for in his line of work he was used to having to prove his agility as well as his prowess with his weaponry.

Carey led the grey into the confines of the livery stable and moved close to the glowing coals. They were still warm and took the chill out of his thirty-year-old bones.

11

The shuffling of boots from the depths of the large interior drew his eyes as he turned to face the unseen man his ears told him was approaching.

The blacksmith was muscular, as were all men of his breed, and just as fragrant. The crimson light of the forge lit up the huge frame as he moved slowly toward Carey.

'Howdy, stranger,' the blacksmith said as he rested a large tin cup down on the coals.

'Howdy.' Carey lowered his hand away from the holstered Colt when he was convinced that the massive man was no threat. He nodded at the blacksmith as the man rested a hip on the edge of the forge. 'Can you fit my grey in here for a couple of days?'

The blacksmith eyed up the stallion with admiration. 'Reckon I could squeeze that fine critter in here.'

Carey pulled a few silver dollars from his vest pocket and handed them to the seated man, who was stirring the black beverage in his cup with a well-chewed pencil. He untied his saddlebags, lay the satchels over his shoulder and walked to the wide-open doors.

He paused and looked back at the blacksmith. 'Where's the hotel, friend?'

The blacksmith raised his head. 'Right next to the sheriff's office.'

Carey inhaled deeply and touched his hat brim.

'Much obliged,' he said.

Carey walked out into the darkness. He could still feel the heat of the glowing coals on his back as he glanced up and down Front Street. It was so dark that it was hard to read any of the painted façades but there was a glowing light down the opposite end of the long street.

He had not seen it before because he had ridden in from the southern end of town. He turned on his heels and walked silently toward it.

Unlike the majority of men who rode the West, Rex Carey did not use spurs. He had learned long ago that spurs had a tendency to jingle and men like Carey did not care for anyone to know where they were.

13

His Cuban-heeled boots made no noise as they walked through the sand toward the lamplight that spilled out from the building Carey assumed must be the hotel.

He was right. The hotel was larger than a town like Willow Creek deserved, but it was the building right next to it that caused Carey to stop in his tracks and ponder.

The tall, elegant figure rested and stared at the locked-up sheriff's office. He rubbed his jaw and then continued the short walk to the boardwalk. Lamplight escaped from the glass panes of the hotel's double doors.

Carey gripped the brass handle, turned it and entered.

It was a fine lobby. Again, it seemed far too grand to be found in a remote town like Willow Creek. Carey walked across the well-trodden carpet to the desk and rested his left hand upon the highly polished surface of the finely carved mahogany.

There seemed to be no one about the

vast lobby. Carey stared at the mail-holes and the score of keys hanging from hooks beneath each of them.

It did not seem to make any sense to Carey. He wondered why a ramshackle town like this would have such a fine hotel. He glanced around the lobby. Everything was perfect. The wallpaper was fresh; the paintwork neatly executed; the drapes were cleaner than any he had ever seen.

Someone had not only spent a lot of money building the hotel, but had also wasted even more decorating it.

Carey tapped his palm down on the bell placed next to the register and inkwell. He had hit the bell four times when he saw a man emerge from a large room and walk toward him. The man had baggy eyes as all men who spent their nights riding a hotel night-desk tend to have.

'Greetings, friend,' said the man, as though he were reciting from a script. He rounded the desk, plucked the pen from its holder and offered it to Carey. 'Room?'

'Yep!' Carey accepted the pen as the register was spun around for him to sign. He dipped the nib into the inkwell and then scrawled his name across the vacant line. As he wrote his eyes read every other name which preceded it. His left eyebrow rose as he straightened up to his full height and looked at the clerk.

The far smaller man looked at Carey curiously.

'Is anything wrong?' he nervously enquired before glancing down at the drying name on his register. 'Mr Carey.'

'Nope,' Carey said. 'Nothing's wrong.'

The nervous clerk tilted his head and looked hard at the register again. After years of practice he was well used to reading upside-down, yet no matter how hard he stared he could not understand the strange expression etched on the face of his latest guest.

'What have you found that's so interesting?' he wondered out loud.

Carey curled his fingers around the grip of his .45 and narrowed his stare.

He pointed to the name three lines above his own on the register, then looked up into the face of the clerk.

'When did Zane Black sign out of this fine hotel?' he drawled in a low whisper.

The clerk felt his throat tighten. He suddenly remembered where he had heard the name of Rex Carey.

'You're the Gun Master,' he gasped. 'I've read all about you, Mr Carey. You're the Gun Master. You're the famous bounty hunter.'

'I ain't no bounty hunter,' Carey disagreed. 'I kill only those that need killing. There's a difference.'

The clerk stared with admiring eyes at the man before him. 'But I thought you hunted the critters with bounty on their heads. That's mighty brave.'

'Like I said,' Carey repeated, 'I only kill those that need killing.'

The clerk wiped the sweat from his brow. 'I understand.'

Carey ignored the sickening admiration and jabbed his finger on to the register.

'I asked you when Black signed out of this hotel, *amigo*,' Carey pressed. 'I'd appreciate an answer.'

The clerk looked confused and pointed to the carpeted staircase in a sweeping gesture.

'But Mr Black is still here, Mr Carey,' he answered. 'I believe he's up in his room right now.'

Rex Carey exhaled and handed his saddlebags to the far shorter man. 'Look after my bags for a little while. I got me business with Zane Black.'

'What kind of business?'

Carey raised an eyebrow. 'Permanent business.'

The expression on the clerk's face altered as he realized what the hotel's new guest meant.

'Oh,' he muttered.

'Keep them bags safe, *amigo*.'

'Certainly.' The smaller man gulped.

'Room eight?' Carey checked as he aimed his trim frame at the staircase and adjusted his gun-belt.

'Room eight is Mr Black's room.' The

clerk placed the bags at his feet behind the desk. 'Is he expecting you, sir?'

A wry smile traced Carey's profile as he started toward the wide flight of steps.

'I surely hope not,' he replied.

2

The corridor on the landing was well lit. Three wall lamps glowed as Carey strode silently toward the red door set at the far end. The brass number 8 lured the tall man like a moth drawn to a bright flame. He pushed his coat-tail over his holster and kept on walking. His right hand rested upon his holstered gun as its digits curled around the ivory grip of its handle.

He moved like a puma. There was no sound in his steps as his boots travelled along the lush carpet toward his goal. His unblinking eyes stared at the door whilst his mind imagined what rested behind the solid wood.

Zane Black was one of the most dangerous gunmen in the territory and was well known for killing anyone if his price was met. Black was everything Carey despised. He was a hired killer who had somehow managed to avoid the law and be branded a merciless killer.

Carey paused before the red door. He licked his lips and inhaled deeply as he listened to the snoring.

There was only one certain way to kill someone like Black, he told himself. That was to kick the door down and start shooting as soon as he saw his target, but Carey was no ruthless killer like the man on the other side of the crimson obstacle.

He was the Gun Master.

Even though it meant that he risked his very life, he always gave his enemies a warning. He always offered them the chance of bettering him. So far his expertise with his six-shooter had never let him down.

He looked down the dark corridor. Every door was locked and bolted. None of the guests knew that soon their slumber would be interrupted. Carey slowly raised his left hand as his right continued to hold on to his holstered six-shooter. He rapped the door twice.

The snoring stopped.

Carey listened to the movement within the room. He could hear the grunts and the sound of feet on the room floor as Black abruptly threw himself out of bed.

He heard three plodding steps and the sound of metal being drawn from leather.

Carey stepped aside. He knew that the deadly hired killer had found his weapon and pulled it free of its holster. The sound of its gun hammer being cocked resonated from the interior of room eight.

'Who is it?' Black snarled.

'Rex Carey.'

'The Gun Master?' The name was enough to rid Black of every scrap of sleep that had pervaded his mind. His eyes narrowed as he aimed his gun at the door. 'Eat lead, Carey.'

The room rocked as bullets tore from his gun barrel and hit the two-inch-thick wooden door. The red door was ripped apart by the fearsome gunfire. Splinters filled the long corridor as Carey rested against the wall.

The Gun Master swiftly drew his own .45, swung around and kicked the door handle as hard as he could. The door was torn from its hinges and flew into the darkness as the eyes of both men locked on to one another.

Deafening flashes lit up the room as Black squeezed his trigger over and over again. Carey dropped on to his knees beside the door frame as red-hot tapers of lethal lead whizzed over his head. He saw the gunfighter reach for his other holstered gun.

Carey fanned his hammer three times. He watched as smoke and lethal tapers burst from his own six-shooter and homed in on Black.

Even the blinding gunsmoke could not fool Carey's senses as to the result of his firing. A noise filled his ears. It was the unmistakable sound of a body hitting the floor hard.

Carey rose back up to his full height

and moved silently into the room with his six-shooter still aimed at the dead body. When he reached Black he looked down at the three perfectly placed bullet-holes in the hired killer's naked chest. Blood pumped from each of the holes.

The Gun Master plucked the spent casings from his smoking chambers as his narrowed eyes continued to glare down at the dead Zane Black.

'Reckon it's time you retired, Black,' he muttered before turning and walking back toward the door. Every door along the corridor opened and people of every shape and size emerged from their rooms to find out what had dragged them from their dreams so abruptly.

Carey walked silently between them. As he headed back to the staircase the crowd cautiously moved to the smoke-filled room and the corpse, which lay in a pool of its own blood beside the bed.

3

There was no hint of emotion upon the handsome features of Carey as he descended the flight of steps back down to the hotel lobby. He strode toward the desk and lifted his left hand and accepted his saddlebags from the clerk. The shaking man stood before the tall gunfighter, open-mouthed as Carey hoisted the bags and balanced them over his wide frame.

The clerk swallowed hard and then managed to utter a few words. 'I heard shooting,' he mumbled.

Carey gave a slow nod of his head and then pulled a slim cigar case from his inside coat pocket.

'That would be me and Black having a disagreement, *amigo*.' The lid of the silver case sprang open and Carey withdrew a long, slim, black cigar and placed it between his teeth. 'We settled our score now.'

The clerk struck a match and lifted it. 'Settled it?'

'Yep. Settled it.' Carey inhaled smoke from the cigar and then blew the match flame out. He closed the case and slid it back into the pocket just as a handful of the hotel guests appeared at the top of the stairs. He stepped to the side of the clerk and rested a hip against a stool as irate people came down the staircase. 'Looks like you got a mutiny on your hands, *amigo*.'

As the crowd gathered around the totally confused clerk, Carey noticed the tin star in the doorway. Sheriff Will Hume stood nervously holding a cocked carbine in his hands as his eyes surveyed the angry hotel guests shouting at the bemused clerk.

Then he saw Carey and straightened up. His hands clutched the rifle as he advanced toward the gunfighter. As some of the guests approached the lawman he brushed them aside. He was not interested in anyone apart from the stranger.

Carey watched Hume through cigar

smoke. There was still no sign of any emotion upon his chiselled features as the sheriff reached him.

Hume waved the rifle at Carey. There was no doubt that Hume was willing to use his trusty weapon at any moment.

'Did you have anything to do with them shots that woke me up, stranger?' the sheriff growled.

Carey pulled the cigar from his lips and smiled.

'I fired half them shots, Sheriff,' he admitted.

Hume looked stunned by the admission. 'Who fired the other half?'

'The dead man in room eight,' Carey said as he watched the clerk vainly trying to console the angry and bewildered guests.

The sheriff had never known anyone freely admit that they had gunned down anyone before. He was startled by the totally disinterested man before him. He edged closer to Carey.

Hume frowned. 'You killed him?'

Carey nodded and sucked more smoke

from his cigar. 'I sure did. I always reckon it pays to shoot back when someone is trying to kill you. It also pays to kill them otherwise they just up and keep shooting.'

'Who did you kill?'

'Zane Black.'

Hume pushed the rifle barrel into the chest of the seated man and growled. 'I don't care for folks that go around shooting other folks in my town, son. Who in tarnation are you anyway?'

Carey rose up and dropped the cigar into an ashtray.

'My name's Rex Carey,' he said.

Sheriff Hume reeled back when he heard the name. Although he had never set eyes upon the tall figure before him, he had heard the name many times.

'You're the Gun Master.'

Carey silently moved through the crowd of half-dressed people toward the staircase. He placed a boot on the bottom step and then looked back at the sheriff.

'That's right, Sheriff,' he agreed. 'Some folks call me that.'

The faces of the hotel's guests suddenly darted between the lawman and the stationary figure ready to ascend the staircase. There was an unnerving silence that filled the foyer. The crowd separated until there was nothing between Hume and Carey.

Carey watched as the hesitant sheriff walked toward him.

'You do realize that I could arrest you, Carey,' Hume said nervously as he reached the tall man. 'Even the legendary Gun Master can't go about killing just anyone he takes a dislike to, boy. Murder is murder, and we got us a real fine oak tree with mighty strong branches. A heap of folks have had their necks stretched on them branches afore now.'

Carey ran a hand over his slim neck as his eyes burned down into the face of the lawman. He smiled and gave a shake of his head.

'You can't hang an innocent man, Sheriff,' he said.

'How do I know you're innocent?' Hume sighed.

'It was self-defence and that ain't a hanging offence,' Carey informed his accuser.

Hume moved even closer and looked up into the eyes of the man who was glaring at him. 'But you can see my problem. I've only your word that it was self-defence, boy.'

'Wrong,' Carey said. 'The door on room eight can prove I'm telling the truth.'

The wrinkled face of Hume looked pained. 'What?'

Carey tilted his head. 'C'mon. Follow me. I'll show you.'

The sheriff trailed the Gun Master up the lush carpeted staircase toward the landing. There was no sign that Carey was either concerned or troubled as he reached the landing and pointed at the door at the end of the well-lit passageway between the other room doors.

Hume rested his hands on his gun belt and stared through the gunsmoke, which still lingered. He could see the door hanging upon its hinges.

'See them bullet-holes?' Carey asked before looking at the lawman. 'They're proof that Black fired first. He heard me call out his name and then blasted his hog leg at the door. I kicked the door in and he fired again. I then killed him. That ain't murder.'

'Why did you go to his room in the first place, Carey?' Hume asked. 'Seems to me that you had killing in mind.'

'I'd heard that Black wanted me dead, Sheriff,' Carey explained. 'So I figured I'd give him the chance to fulfil his wish.'

Hume raised a bushy eyebrow. 'It seems to me that you were right. Black sure wanted you dead for some reason.'

'And he failed,' Carey stated. 'It don't pay to slap leather against me.'

Hume gave a nod of his head. 'Reckon not.'

'Well, then, if that's all I'll be heading to my bed.' Carey checked the number on his room key and then turned on his heels and started toward another of the numerous doors.

Sheriff Hume watched as the famed Gun Master slid his key into the lock and entered the hotel room. The sound of the bolt being slid across filled the quiet landing as the lawman glanced at room eight and the remains of Zane Black sprawled across the blood stained floor. He exhaled and moved to the landing railings. Every one of the people below him was looking up at him.

'Get the undertaker, Clem boy!' Hume shouted down at the clerk. 'Tell him to get here fast. I want that dead 'un hauled out of here before the flies wake up.'

4

The resounding noise of horses' hoofs echoed all around the clearing as the horsemen carved their way through the dense undergrowth as they travelled through the moonlit countryside toward their goal. The sound of prairie hens scattering caused the five dust-caked horsemen to draw rein and rest as the lead rider dropped from his saddle and knelt down. He brushed the loose grass aside and glared down at the churned-up ground.

'What you seen, Forrest?' one of the riders asked.

'We ain't the only critters to have ridden through here in the last few hours,' Forrest Black said. He stood back up and bit his lower lip thoughtfully. 'Somebody else is headed to Willow Creek, boys.'

Just like his brother Zane, Forrest was a skilled gunfighter who hired his talents out to anyone that could afford his price. He was also a ruthless bank robber but, like the men that followed him, he had never been caught.

'Do you figure we got us competition, Forrest?'

'Nope.' Black pulled his canteen from the saddle horn and unscrewed its stopper as his eyes watched his four companions. None of them could be trusted but they were good at what they did and what they did was kill. He raised the canteen to his lips and added, 'I reckon that whoever it is riding toward Willow Creek ain't gonna give us no grief.'

As Black drank, Bob Edwards, Slim Darren, Don Holly and Eli Monk watched their leader with fearful eyes. They were killers, but Black had been cast from a different mould. Unlike the merciless Black, they were not cursed by the constant and insane mood swings that had haunted all of the Black clan over the years. What Forrest Black did not realize as he consumed the last droplets of his canteen was that he was now the only remaining member of his once large family.

The gunfighter wiped his mouth along his sleeve and returned the canteen to his saddle horn and then moved toward his men. Even the moonlight could not hide the irrational fever which fermented in his depraved mind.

'Whoever left them tracks must just be headed to the same place as us,' Darren said as he leaned over the mane of his mount. 'Ain't that right, Forrest?'

Black gave a nod. 'Yep, Slim. Nothing to fret about.'

Monk screwed up his eyes and stared through the moonlight at the eerie landscape that confronted them. 'This is the second time we've come across tracks heading to Willow Creek, Forrest. Do you figure it's the same *hombre?*'

Black gave a shrug. 'It might be.'

Holly looked at Monk. 'Stop worrying, Eli. Forrest's brother sent for us. Nobody else knows anything about the job he's got lined up for us. Them tracks don't mean nothing.'

Black placed his hands on his gun grips. His men fell silent as they observed his familiar action. They knew that the man who led them was about to speak and it was unhealthy to interrupt him.

'We're going to Willow Creek just like Zane told us to do,' Black said in a low growl. 'You boys are plumb jumpy. You're scared of your own shadows.'

Edwards nodded. 'Forrest's right. We're all getting jumpy.'

Black stared at the moonlit treeline ahead of them. He looked back at his followers and gave a sickening grin. 'I got me a feeling that by this time tomorrow we'll be up to our chins in gold coin, boys.'

Darren looked nervous as he stared down at the disturbed ground before them. 'Reckon them hoof tracks were left by a drummer looking for some-place to sell his goods. The dude can't give us no trouble.'

Black narrowed his eyes. 'Damn right, Slim. It's probably just some drummer heading to Willow Creek.'

The riders all started to nod in agreement.

'All we got to think about is this.' Black drew his horse closer and reached up for the saddle horn. 'My brother telegraphed me and told me of a real juicy bank job that he's got planned for us. When Zane reckons there's an easy bank to be skinned, there is. Zane never steers me wrong.'

Monk gritted his teeth. 'When we were in Laredo I heard tales that the Gun Master was looking for your brother, Forrest.'

Black-eyed Monk smiled. 'I heard them same stories, Eli. That varmint don't know how fast Zane is with his guns. He'll soon find out if he tussles with him, though.'

Edwards rubbed his unshaven jaw. 'You don't figure them tracks could belong to the Gun Master, do you?'

'Bob, I vowed I'd kill the Gun Master

if he makes a play for me or Zane,' Black snarled as he waved his clenched fists at his men. 'I don't want to hear any more of your wild theories about who left them tracks. I'll kill any of you just like I'll kill the Gun Master if you keep gabbing.'

Bob Edwards edged his mount closer to Black. 'We signed on to join you and your brother Zane in robbing a bank, Forrest. You never mentioned anything about the Gun Master.'

Faster than any of them had ever seen anyone draw a gun from its holster before, Black swiftly drew one of his weapons and fanned its hammer. A deafening blast spewed from the gun barrel. A bullet tore through the eerie moonlight and ripped a chunk out of Edwards' ear. Blood and skin sprayed over the moonlit clearing as Edwards screamed out in horror.

Black stared at the others with unblinking eyes.

'Just remember that the next bullet could be splitting any of your skulls in half, boys,' Black warned them. 'I ain't in no mood to nurse-feed you varmints. We're going to rob us a bank in Willow Creek. Savvy?'

They all nodded fearfully.

Black rammed his smoking gun back into its holster, threw himself up on top of his saddle and gathered up his reins. His eyes burned through the moonlight at Edwards as the wounded man tried to stem the bleeding of his mutilated ear.

The ruthless leader of the riders spat at the ground and jabbed his spurs into the flesh of his mount.

'C'mon. We got us a bank to strip naked.' He roared with laughter as his horse continued on toward Willow Creek.

They all followed Black through the moonlit brush. They were too afraid to do anything else.

5

The smell of carbolic soap filled the entire hotel as Rex Carey felt the sun start to move across his face. His eyes opened and then shied away. He kicked off the bed sheets and lowered his legs on to the cold surface of the floor before rising. He inhaled the scent of the aromatic soap which had been used to wash away all evidence of death from the hotel. But to those who had heard and witnessed the result of the deadly gunplay, it was a vain attempt.

There were some things that not even the strongest carbolic soap could erase. The memory of the Gun Master's prowess was one of them.

Carey poured water into a bowl from the pitcher on the night-stand and quickly washed all remnants of sleep from his face. He wiped his face dry and then moved back to the bed and his clothes. After he had dressed Carey lifted his gun-belt off the bedpost and swung it around his waist.

Carey buckled the belt and carefully adjusted the holster until his .45 hung on his right hip. He secured the long leather laces around his thigh before lifting up his hat and placing it on to his still-damp hair.

The Gun Master was ready for a new day. He picked up his bags and unbolted the door before stepping back out on to the landing.

The sight of men working busily confused him for a moment. Carey watched as a handful of tradesmen milled around the corridor. As he reached the top of the staircase he glanced back at room eight.

A new door had replaced the battered one and all evidence of the duel he and Zane Black had fought within the room's confines were gone.

He shook his head and then continued down to the foyer.

Without pausing he headed straight

to the desk and stared at the slumbering clerk. He clenched a fist and pounded the bell beside the register. The sound caused the clerk to leap off his chair. Clem Jones stared at the tall man across the desk from him and gave a slow, respectful nod.

'Howdy, Mr Carey,' he said.

Carey touched the brim of his hat. 'Howdy, *amigo*.'

'What can I do for you?'

'Two things, *amigo*,' Carey replied. 'The first is to tell me where I might find a certain Judge Oliver and the second is to get my horse from the livery.'

Carey tossed a few silver dollars on to the desk.

The young clerk was thoughtful for a moment.

'The judge lives on a cattle spread just east of town,' he said as he scooped up the coins. 'It's an hour ride there and back.'

'I ain't in no hurry.' Carey nodded.

'I'll send a bellhop to get your horse

for you.' Jones stepped from behind the desk. 'What kinda nag is it?'

'It's a grey stallion.' Carey turned away from the desk and swung his saddlebags on to his wide shoulder. 'Tell your bellhop to bring it to the café yonder. I'll be waiting.'

Clem Jones watched as Carey strode out of the hotel and made his way across the quiet street. The early-morning sunshine glinted on his holstered six-shooter. The clerk shrugged.

'I sure wish I was a Gun Master like him,' he sighed, and then caught sight of himself in one of the hotel's many mirrors. The truth dawned on him. He shook his head and made his way to the staff quarters in search of one of the hotel's many bellhops.

Rex Carey could smell the fragrant aroma of cooking even before he turned the door handle and entered the café. He removed his Stetson and stood for a moment studying the empty establishment. Then a handsome female emerged from a back room through a curtain of beads. She looked around thirty with long dark hair, which reached her waist. Carey was stunned by her natural beauty and smiled at her. She looked at him and was unable to conceal her surprise. She had thought that she had seen every man in Willow Creek but was pleasantly surprised to be proven wrong.

Without her even realizing it, her hands brushed loose strands of hair from her face.

'Any chance of breakfast, ma'am?' Carey asked as he glanced around the empty café. 'I know it's early.'

'If you're hungry, it's never too early.'

Carey allowed her to pass him and make her way through the chairs and tables toward the window.

'This is the best table in here,' she said.

He grinned and silently followed. 'Much obliged.'

Sally Quinn smiled and gestured to the table closest to the window. He sat down.

'What exactly do you want to eat?' she asked.

Carey saw a youngster running from the hotel. The bellhop was headed in the direction he had left his prized horse the night before.

She cleared her throat. Carey looked at her.

'I'm sorry, ma'am,' he apologized. 'Eggs and bread will do just fine.'

Sally looked at the stranger. She had never seen him before and yet there was something about Carey that seemed to tell her that she ought to recognize him.

'Do you want coffee?' she asked.

He placed his saddlebags down on the empty chair next to him and then dropped his hat over the satchels.

'Thank you kindly, ma'am,' he said. 'I am a tad thirsty now you mention it.'

Sally was about to return to her kitchen when something caused her to stop and stare at her newest customer. 'I know this sounds loco but do I know you, mister?'

Carey looked at her. He smiled.

'I don't think so but I wish I was wrong, ma'am,' he replied.

'My name's Sally.' She blushed and then hurriedly pushed her way through the beaded curtain.

Carey watched as the beads swayed back and forth. For the first time in years he had actually met someone who interested him. A female that was not covered in powder and face paint like so many others he was used to meeting on his travels.

He pulled out his cigar case and opened it. As his fingers gripped one of the slim black smokes he noticed something from the window.

It was dust rising from the distant hills.

Carey stood. 'That's a lot of hoof dust.'

Sally walked back from the kitchen and placed the cup of black coffee down on the table before him. She could see the concern in his face.

'What's wrong?' she asked.

He looked at her. 'Maybe nothing, ma'am.'

'I told you — my name's Sally,' she

said before adding, 'What's eating you?'

He raised a hand and pointed at the distant hills. 'You expecting a stage-coach in town?'

Sally Quinn looked to where he was indicating and frowned for a few moments. 'The only stage that arrives here in Willow Creek comes on Saturday. If you ask me that's riders. A bunch of them.'

Carey sighed. 'That's what I was thinking.'

She watched as he sipped his coffee. 'How come you look so concerned about a bunch of riders headed here, handsome?'

He finished the coffee and rubbed his jaw. 'It's a long story, Sally. Even I don't know all of it yet.'

For the first time since she was an innocent youth Sally felt drawn to the stranger. Her long fingers touched his face and focused his attention on her.

'What's your name?' she asked.

Carey swallowed hard. 'My name's Rex Carey.'

Sally clutched at her apron. 'The Gun Master?'

He nodded. 'That's what folks have tagged me.'

'I've heard a lot of stories about you, Rex,' Sally said softly. 'They say that there ain't anyone as skilful with his gun as you are.'

Carey looked away from her gaze. 'There's always someone out there that's a little faster and more accurate with his gun, Sally.'

'Maybe you ought to quit while you still can,' she advised.

'There ain't much I can do besides shooting, Sally,' Carey said. 'A lot of folks rely on me to protect them from varmints.'

Sally looked saddened and disappointed.

'I'll get your eggs, Rex,' she told him.

Carey watched her walk back to her kitchen. For the first time in a long while the Gun Master felt uneasy. He finished his coffee and placed a couple of silver dollars on the chequered table-cloth.

Without making a sound he rose

from his chair and gathered up his things.

As Sally came through the beaded drapes with a plate of eggs in her hand she saw that Carey was gone. She rushed to the window, placed the plate down upon the table and looked out into the street.

There was no sign of the handsome man anywhere.

'Damn it all!' Sally cursed angrily. 'The only good-looking man that's walked in here and I have to scare him off.'

She was about to pick up the empty cup when she noticed the cloud of hoof dust on the hillside again. Sally squinted and started to count the approaching horsemen.

'Five riders,' she said aloud as her thoughts returned to Carey. 'Why do I have this feeling inside me that they'll be waging war on Rex before the sun goes down?'

She felt her heart quicken.

6

The five horsemen gathered pace as they navigated the last mile toward Willow Creek. The scent of civilization drew them off the tree-covered hills like flies to an outhouse. Forrest Black led his band of cut-throats down the dusty slopes and into the outskirts of the barely awake settlement. There was an urgency in the lead rider that had grown stronger the closer he had gotten to the town.

Black pulled back on his long leathers as the hoofs of their mounts found level ground. The rest of the deadly gang drew level with Black and looked to his determined face for any sign of emotion.

There was none.

All that was carved in his craggy features was bitter loathing for every man, woman or child they rode past.

Black did not move as he allowed his horse to canter through the labyrinth of streets toward the long main thoroughfare.

His dark eyes darted from one of the townsfolk to another as though in search for someone to kill. His four outriders knew that was exactly what he wanted to do.

Should any of the innocent faces cast their eyes upon Black and allow their curiosity to linger too long, he would erupt like a volcano.

There was no reason in him. There had not been for more than a year. His mind no longer functioned like most other minds and seemed to be getting worse with each new dawn.

The sun was still low as Black turned the corner into the main street. He glanced to both sides of him as he and his men closed the distance between themselves and the livery stable.

The five horsemen stopped their horses outside the wide-open doors of the livery and dismounted. Black stared at the tall, weathered structure and then swung on his heels to face the street.

His men surrounded him as he brooded.

'What we gonna do now?' Monk asked as he held the five sets of reins in his gloved hands.

Edwards held his hand to his ear as blood seeped through the gaps between his fingers.

'I'm getting my ear sewed up,' he grunted.

Black glanced at Edwards and sneered. 'Go get your damn ear tended, Bob. I'd hate for you to be crying like an old hag when we're robbing the bank.'

'Good idea, Forrest.' Edwards spotted a wooden shingle with 'Doc Smith' painted upon its varnished surface. He walked toward it.

Black looked at Monk. 'Take the horses in the stable. Buy fresh mounts and switch our saddles and bridles, Eli.'

Monk sheepishly obeyed.

Black rested his hands on his holstered guns as Darren and Holly closed in on their erratic leader. Like their cohorts, they were not about to question Black's orders.

'We have to find the hotel,' Black reasoned as he rubbed his unshaven jaw. 'Yeah, that's what we do first.'

'Good idea, Forrest,' Holly muttered.

Darren pointed to the far end of the street. 'I reckon we might find a hotel down that way, Forrest.'

Black nodded. 'I reckon you're right, Slim. C'mon. We have to find my brother. We have to find out what he has planned for us. Zane always has real smart plans brewing in his head.'

As Monk stood by the lofty doors of the livery he watched Edwards disappear into the doctor's surgery and Black leading Darren and Holly down the street. He gave a sigh and turned back to face the blacksmith.

'You look troubled, son,' the blacksmith noted as he pulled a saddle from the back of one of their horses.

'I am, mister,' Monk admitted. 'More damn troubled than I care to admit.'

53

'How come?'

Monk rubbed the tails of his bandana over his dust-covered face and shrugged. Even when Black was out of earshot the deadly young killer was afraid of him.

'Hurry up and get me five fresh nags, old-timer,' he said.

Black noticed every storefront that he and the two men who flanked him passed. His eyes darted like daggers to each and every one of them. Then, to the surprise of both Darren and Holly, Black abruptly stopped and turned. He stared as though haunted by unseen ghosts at the fancy funeral parlour with its windows decked in yards of black silk.

'What's wrong, Forrest?' Holly asked.

Black was standing like a statue staring at the window of the undertaker's office and showroom. He then shook as though he had felt an imaginary cold breeze.

'You OK, Forrest?' Darren asked, nervously.

Black slowly tilted his head and

stared at both his men in turn. His face was ashen. Somehow he managed to start walking again toward the hotel.

'The hotel is up yonder.' Holly pointed.

Black did not speak. He just kept walking toward the building that his underling had pointed to. The men who followed Forrest Black had never seen him like this before. It worried them.

They were about fifty yards from the hotel when Black stopped again and inhaled deeply.

'I'm thirsty,' he said, unexpectedly, then turned to stare at the shuttered and locked doors of a saloon. 'We're gonna get us a drink. A real big drink.'

Darren watched as Black stepped up from the street and stood outside the locked doors of the Mustang Saloon. He and Holly moved up to the boardwalk.

'We're thirsty as well but it's damn early, Forrest,' Darren said. 'Reckon it'll be open after we meet up with your brother.'

Black either did not hear the words or chose to ignore them. His head moved back and forth on his long neck as he glared at the solid doors.

Then he drew one of his six-shooters and cocked its hammer and levelled it at the brass lock. The deafening sound of a bullet being fired filled the length of the street. He cocked his hammer again and then squeezed the trigger.

The lock and part of the wooden door fell to the floor as Black kicked the double doors into the saloon. He then entered.

Darren and Holly raced in after Black. They watched as he plucked the spent casings from his smoking .45 and replaced them with fresh cartridges from his belt.

Black's deathly glare was fixed on his cohorts. 'Get us some bottles of whiskey, boys.'

They obeyed and rushed behind the long, mahogany bar counter and pulled three of the most expensive whiskey bottles from a shelf. They stood the bottles on the counter and then jumped over to where Black was standing.

Black was holding the hot gun in his hand and watching the gunsmoke trail from its barrel.

'You ever had a real bad feeling in your craw, boys?' Black asked them as he rested on a bar stool.

'What kind of bad feeling?' Holly wondered as he pulled the cork from one of the bottles and raised its neck to his dry lips.

'The kind of feeling you just can't explain,' Black continued as he watched the smoke. 'I had me the strangest feeling when I saw that funeral parlour. It was like being kicked by a mule.'

Both his men shook their heads.

Black was about to explain further when his attention was drawn to the doorway they had just entered by. His expression seemed to harden as he stepped away from the counter.

'Who is that?' Black shouted out at the figure by the door. 'Show yourself!'

Holly and Darren lowered the bottles

from their mouths as they saw the glinting of the tin star.

Black straightened and then watched as Will Hume came into the Mustang with his Winchester held across his chest. The lawman stopped when he was within twenty feet of Black.

'What's your game, boys?' Hume asked. 'Folks in Willow Creek don't like it when strangers bust into their saloons and steal drink.'

A rage swelled up inside Black. He started to twitch as he continued to stare at the smoking gun in his hand. He raised his free hand and pushed the brim of his hat off his brow.

'You talking to me, Sheriff?' Black asked.

Hume gave a quick nod of his head. 'Yep.'

'I was thirsty and we've ridden a long way,' Black hissed as he turned to face the lawman. 'Ain't our fault that the saloon owners are plumb lazy. If they opened up earlier we'd not have had to bust in here.'

Hume turned the barrel of his Winchester until it was aimed straight at Black.

'Drop them guns and raise your arms,' he said.

Black started to laugh. It was not the laughter of someone who had just heard a joke. It was the sickening sound only madmen can muster.

'You skilled at killing, Sheriff?' Black asked.

The lawman was taken aback by the question. He could see that Black, unlike his associates, was unafraid. Even with a cocked rifle aimed straight at his belly, Black was totally unafraid.

'Don't get smart, boy,' Hume said. 'Drop them guns.'

'What for?' Black was now staring straight into the wrinkled eyes of the lawman. His smile and laughter grew more intense. 'You figuring on killing me?'

Hume licked his lips. They were dry.

'You're under arrest,' he said.

Black shook his head.

'I'm not going anywhere until I've had my drink,' he said.

'Who are you?' Hume asked the unconcerned Black as his hands started to shake nervously. 'What are you doing in my town?'

'The name's Forrest Black, Sheriff,' the gunfighter answered before adding, 'My brother sent for us. We were just on our way to meet up with him when I got thirsty.'

Hume's expression altered. 'You say your name's Black?'

'Yep.'

'Does your brother go by the name of Zane?' the lawman asked.

'That's him.' Black nodded. 'You know him?'

'We've met.' The sheriff began to realize that Forrest Black might not take the knowledge of his sibling's demise too well. He lowered the barrel of the Winchester and started to back away from the three men.

Black raised an eyebrow. 'Where you going, Sheriff?'

Without taking his eyes off Black, Hume continued to retrace his steps back to the doorway.

'I just recalled I've got me an appointment,' he said.

Black and his cronies watched as the lawman moved quickly out into the street. Black turned to Holly and dropped his gun into its holster.

'That was odd,' Black muttered as he picked up a whiskey bottle and drew its cork with his teeth. He spat it at the floor and shook his head. 'That was mighty odd. I never seen anyone move as fast as that critter.'

Darren rubbed his neck. 'That fat old sheriff lost all his colour when you started talking about Zane.'

'He was real spooked,' Holly added.

Black lowered the bottle from his lips. 'But why was he spooked, boys?'

'It don't make no sense.' Holly shrugged. 'Unless he's tangled with your brother and knows how tough he is.'

Black nodded. 'That must be it. That sheriff is scared of Zane and didn't want him getting ornery. My brother does get kinda protective of me.'

Darren chuckled.

'Did you see his face? He thought you was really gonna shoot him, Forrest.'

'He sure did.' Holly grinned as he took a swig of whiskey.

Black stared over his bottle. His ruthless eyes were hollow as they glanced at the spot where Sheriff Hume had been standing.

'The sheriff was right,' Black snarled. 'I was gonna shoot him.'

7

Dust drifted up into the morning sky as Rex Carey drove his grey stallion toward the large ranch house set amid a thousand acres of fertile pasture. He had ridden through a few hundred head of longhorn steers before reaching the Bar O ranch. Carey slowed his mount as he approached the long, white-washed building.

As the powerful grey cantered to a halt beside the ranch house, Carey noticed movement to either side of him. Several cowboys approached as he reined in.

Carey tilted his head and looked to both sides. The cowboys were young and armed. He smiled and carefully dismounted the stallion. He did not utter a word as he looped his long leathers around the hitching pole and secured them firmly.

63

He stood next to the pole and watched as the cowboys got closer. Every one of them had their hands on the grips of their guns. They were ready to draw and Carey was ready to oblige them.

'No need to fret, boys,' Judge Oliver said from behind the broad shoulders of the Gun Master. 'This is a friend of mine. I sent for him. Go back to your chores.'

Carey turned and saw the judge and touched the brim of his hat. 'Howdy, Judge.'

Oliver watched as his men dispersed and then walked to the edge of the porch. He patted Carey on the back.

'I didn't think you'd get here this soon, Rex,' he said.

'I would have been here sooner if I hadn't have run into trouble with a critter named Black.' Carey removed his hat and allowed the sun to warm his brow.

'He's part of the reason I sent for you,' Oliver said.

'He'll not trouble you any longer.' Carey turned and stepped up next to the lawman. He looked around them. 'You've done well for yourself, Judge,' he commented.

'You had a showdown with Black?'

Carey nodded. 'He started shooting and I was forced to kill him. I hope that ain't gonna bring you any trouble, Judge.'

'So do I.' Oliver placed his hand on Carey's shoulder and led him into the ranch house. The interior of the long building was cooler than outside in the blistering morning sun. The stone fireplace drew both men to it. They rested in soft chairs to either side of its cavernous grate.

Carey sat opposite the judge. 'What's all this about, Judge? I recalled Black from years back; when I saw his name on the hotel register I decided to go have a chat with him. I had no idea he was giving you grief. What exactly is wrong around here?'

Judge Oliver sat with his hands

clenched as though in prayer. He moved back and forth on the well-padded chair as though searching for the words to explain why he had sent for the Gun Master.

'I'm waiting, Judge,' Carey said.

Oliver looked straight at his old friend. 'I shouldn't have gotten you involved in this, Rex. This is not your fight and I'm ashamed to have involved you.'

Carey pulled his silver cigar case from his pocket and flicked it open. He slid one of the long thin black smokes from behind the elastic binder and placed it between his lips.

'I'm still waiting, Judge.'

Oliver watched as Carey closed the case and returned it to his inside pocket. He then leaned forward and exhaled.

'Zane Black has been in Willow Creek for nearly three months. He came to town with barely a silver dollar to his name and after a short while he was able to afford to live in the hotel,' Oliver stated. 'How? The hotel has mighty high rates but Black was suddenly able to afford the cost.'

Carey scratched a match and cupped its flame. He inhaled smoke and blew out the match.

'You reckon Black had a sideline?' he asked.

Oliver nodded. 'He must have. He never did an honest day's work since arriving in town and yet suddenly he was splashing money around like it was confetti. Black must have had some sort of crooked deal going on.'

Carey leaned back against the cushion and gripped the cigar in his teeth. 'You must be right but that don't answer my question of why you sent for me.'

'For months I had no idea of what Black was up to but then I discovered his secret,' Oliver announced.

Carey sat forward. 'I know that look you got in your face, Judge. What exactly was Black up to?'

'Zane Black had his stinking fingers in every dirty job known to man, Rex.'

Oliver could hardly contain his anger. 'He was bleeding folks dry.'

'Blackmail?' Carey suggested.

'And every other sickening vice to boot.' Oliver nodded. 'If a man had a secret in his past Black seemed to know about it and he would exploit that knowledge.'

Carey blew a long line of smoke at the floor. 'And he was blackmailing you about some long-lost error of judgement?'

Oliver could remain seated no longer. He rose to his feet and rested his hands on the mantle of the fireplace. His boot kicked at the stone grate as he spoke.

'To my shame, like most grown men, I have a few skeletons in my past that he somehow managed to learn about.' The judge glanced at Carey. 'I too became another of his victims.'

'You paid him to keep quiet?' Carey asked.

Oliver nodded. 'I did.'

Carey looked at the man he had known and respected for more than a decade. He was unable to hide his amazement that Oliver of all people would have anything in his past that he was ashamed of.

'Are you serious, Judge?' he asked. 'You paid Black to keep silent? What on earth could you have done that you're ashamed of?'

Judge Oliver moved around the room like a man trying to out-pace his own shadow. He stopped beside the window and looked out at the rolling pastures before he summoned the courage to turn and face Carey and reply.

'You might not be able to picture it, Rex, but I haven't always been old.' He sighed heavily. 'I once was like you — young and full of vinegar. I've done a lot of things in my time that I now regret. Somehow Zane Black discovered my secret lapse in judgement and started to milk me dry.'

Carey rose and tossed the cigar into the grate. He walked to the side of the judge and also looked out of the window.

'Did you send for me so that I'd call Black out, Judge?' he asked. 'Maybe you figured that he deserved dying in a showdown. Was that it?'

Oliver turned his head. 'I wouldn't risk your life just to save my blushes, Rex.'

'Then why did you wire me?'

The judge shook his head. 'I was hoping that the mere sight of you would scare the critter off. I hoped that when he knew that the Gun Master was in town he might decide to find easier pickings.'

Carey nodded. 'I believe you, Judge. In all the time we've known one another you ain't ever tried to start a fight.'

Oliver gave a slight laugh. 'It seems that you have helped a lot of folks by gunning down that loathsome varmint. Without even knowing it, you have managed to solve a lot of problems.'

The younger man placed his hat upon his head. 'I'm glad to have been of service, Judge. Even though I didn't have a clue that I was doing anything but defend myself.'

'Stay for lunch.' Oliver smiled.

'I can't.'

'Whyever not?'

Carey grinned and shook his head. 'I'd like to but I reckon I'll just ride back to town and pick up some provisions.'

The judge followed Carey out into the sunshine again and watched as the younger man pulled his reins free.

'Are you leaving Willow Creek already?'

'Yep, I'm leaving.' Carey placed a hand on his saddle horn and stepped into his stirrup. He mounted the grey stallion in one fluid action and gathered up his reins. 'There's no reason why I should stay here now. Everything's settled and I've got places to go.'

Judge Oliver looked at Carey long and hard. 'Where have you got to go, Rex? You can't keep on drifting forever. You'll have to settle down someplace.'

Carey smiled and touched the brim

of his hat. 'I was settled once as you recall, Judge. That was before the War. Now there ain't nowhere for me.'

Oliver stepped forward and placed a hand on his friend's arm. 'You take care of yourself, boy. That's an order.'

Carey saluted and turned the head of his stallion.

'*Adios*, old pal.'

Judge Oliver watched the famed rider known as the Gun Master as he steered his high-shouldered mount back toward Willow Creek. As he stood there staring into the heat haze one of his ranch hands strolled up to the judge.

'How do you know that drifter, Judge?' he asked.

Oliver glanced at the youngster. 'We fought in the War together and he saved my bacon more than once.'

'And now he's nothing more than a drifter,' the cowboy said. 'You'd think he'd go home rather than just wandering.'

The judge lowered his head. 'He has to keep drifting.'

'How come, Judge?'

'Everything that boy knew and loved was killed during the conflict.' Oliver sighed before turning back to the ranch house. 'Some folks keep riding because they can't face looking back.'

The cowboy watched as Carey disappeared from view. He then turned and looked at the judge.

'Who is he, Judge?'

Oliver paused. 'Rex Carey is his name but most folks call him the Gun Master.'

8

The nervous lawman watched from across the wide street as the blacksmith saddled the last of the five mounts within the cavernous stable. Hume's wrinkled eyes burned as they studied Eli Monk as the gang member finally led the five freshly saddled mounts out into the blazing sun. Having survived the encounter in the Mustang, the sheriff suddenly realized that Black and his cronies were not alone. Monk had five fresh horses in tow and that fact alone chilled the lawman. Three gun-toting men were bad enough, but five were even worse.

His mind raced. He knew why Black was in town but why had he brought four obviously ruthless gunmen with him?

Hume was about to leave the cover of the alley when he stopped in his tracks.

His eyes stared fearfully at the heavily bandaged Bob Edwards leaving the doc's place. The lawman watched him join his companion.

Sheriff Hume rubbed the sweat from his face and edged closer to the corner of the alley. Although he had no proof, the lawman was convinced that both Edwards and Monk must belong to Forrest Black's retinue of heavily armed followers.

His heart sank.

The sheriff wondered what might happen within the peaceful town if Rex Carey were to suddenly reappear within its boundaries. He knew that at any time the normally quiet Willow Creek would be subjected to the wrath of a grieving brother when Forrest Black learned what had happened to his brother Zane.

Hume resolved that he had to reach Rex Carey. He wondered what the Gun Master would do when he knew that Black's equally loathsome sibling was in town.

Whatever Carey chose to do, Hume knew it would benefit the townsfolk. If he distracted Black and his gang their bullets would be aimed at him, not at any of the locals. If Carey high-tailed it, Black and his men would follow.

Either way Willow Creek would buy itself some time.

The sheriff narrowed his glare. His eyes darted along the street. From where he had carefully positioned himself he had an uninterrupted view of the Mustang Saloon, the hotel and most of the street. Hume was biting on his lower lip as he pushed his ample girth between two large barrels. He watched as both the two strangers milled around the freshly saddled horses.

Hume's mind kept asking himself the same question.

Why were they here?

There was only one answer.

They were here to kill. Nobody carried that amount of weaponry unless they were intent on killing, he thought.

Monk mounted one of the horses

and then Edwards clambered up on to one of the others. Both men held on to the long leathers of the three other saddle horses and began to ride down toward the hotel.

Only when they were well away from the livery stable did the sheriff find the courage to run out from where he had been hiding and cross the wide street. He reached the livery just as the blacksmith came out into the sunshine.

'Get me a horse, Dan,' Hume demanded as he rested his sweat-soaked back against one of the tall doors. 'As fast as you can.'

'You going someplace, Will?' The blacksmith exhaled and then strode back into the dark interior of his stable.

'I'm going to try and find the owner of the grey stallion,' Hume answered, and watched as Monk and Edwards reached the saloon. He felt his guts twist inside him as he saw the riders stop. Then he saw Black emerge into the sunlight with his two cohorts on his heels. All five men talked as they shared

77

bottles of whiskey.

The sheriff could not hear what was being discussed by the distant quintet but knew that it was not mere gossip. Hume was afraid what Black would do when he discovered the fate of his brother. He had to get out of town as quickly as possible and find the famed Gun Master.

'Hurry up,' Hume urged the blacksmith.

'I'm working as fast as I can, Will,' the burly man said as he tightened the cinch strap and lowered the fender. 'I never seen you so all fired up before.'

The sheriff looked at the large man. 'I ain't never been so damn scared before, Dan.'

The blacksmith led out a saddled mare and handed the reins to the lawman. He had never seen Hume move as quickly before. Within a mere few seconds the sheriff had mounted the horse and was turning it.

'Where you going, Will?'

'I told you,' the lawman whispered.

'I'm off after the critter who rides the grey stallion.'

The blacksmith pointed. 'But he went to Judge Oliver's spread, Will. You got that witless nag aimed in the wrong direction.'

Hume looked at the five heavily armed men standing halfway down the main street. 'If you think I'm riding past them varmints, you're mistaken. I'm headed around your livery so I don't get my head blown off.'

The bewildered blacksmith watched as Hume whipped the tail of the horse and thundered away. He scratched his head and wandered back into the livery stable as the sound of horse's hoofs echoed within the massive structure.

He paused beside the forge and raked its coals.

'What the hell's going on around here?' he asked himself.

9

The five gunmen tied the reins of their five new mounts to the hitching rail outside the handsome hotel and then grouped together before entering. Forrest Black glanced around the hotel foyer with gruesome eyes as his four followers trailed him across the carpeted floor toward the desk. Dust fell from each of the men as their spurs rang out. Every stride the five gunfighters made rang out within the spacious lobby. The few hotel guests that were within the luxurious surroundings looked up from their newspapers and stared in horror at Forrest Black and his gang of hand-picked henchmen.

Clem Jones was awoken from his catnap by the sound of the jangling spurs. He blinked and rubbed the sleep from his eyes, and then jumped up from his chair behind the desk.

The clerk stood with shaking legs behind the desk as his hands nervously tried to remain still upon the large register. He was afraid at what he saw as Black reached the desk and stared down at him.

Jones tried to smile but every muscle in his face refused to obey. He gulped and began to nervously nod at the sight before him.

The gunfighters who flanked Black watched the people who stared at them. Each of them kept their hands on the grips of their holstered guns.

Black leaned over the desk and lowered his head. His eyes burned into Jones like branding irons.

'My name's Black,' he said. 'Forrest Black.'

The name alone chilled the young clerk to the bone. His face began to twitch uncontrollably as he nodded.

'Greetings, Mr Black,' Jones croaked.

Black rested a hand on the desk as his other swung the register around so that he could read the names that filled the page. He ran a fingernail down the names until he found what he was looking for.

His eyes darted back at Jones. 'I see my brother is here.'

The clerk shuffled his feet.

'Ah, not exactly, Mr Black,' he stammered.

Forrest Black screwed up his eyes. 'What do you mean? This is my brother's writing. He's here.'

Jones went to back away but Black's long reach grabbed his coat collar and hauled him closer. The clerk could smell the whiskey fumes on Black's breath. He gulped again as he felt his feet being dragged off the floor.

'Your brother ain't here anymore,' Jones whispered.

Black tightened his grip. 'Where is he, then?'

It felt like a lifetime to the young hotel clerk as he tried desperately to think of an answer that might not send the man who held him in check into a mindless frenzy.

'Answer me.' Black shook Jones violently.

'Your brother had himself an accident,' Jones said as his head rocked on its neck.

The other men closed in on the shoulders of Black as he stopped shaking the defenceless clerk.

'What kinda accident?' Black growled as he pressed his face into Jones's ear. 'A bad'un?'

Jones swallowed hard. 'A real bad'un, sir.'

Black relaxed his grip and watched as the clerk fell backwards into his chair. His eyes focused on the fearful youngster. He tilted his head.

'Where's Zane?' he asked.

Jones was shaking like a leaf ready to fall from a tree branch. He looked at his knees and managed to answer the probing question.

'He's in the funeral parlour.'

Black was about to ask why when he suddenly knew the answer. He placed the palms of his hands on the desk and looked down at the cowering clerk.

'He's dead?'

Jones nodded. 'I'm afraid so, Mr Black.'

'How?' Black snarled as he somehow managed to contain his anger. 'How did my brother get himself killed?'

The clerk shrugged. 'He and Rex Carey had themselves a showdown. Your brother was a tad slower on the draw, I hear.'

'The Gun Master!' Black muttered as he recognized the name of Carey.

'That's him, sir.'

Forrest Black gritted his teeth and pulled both his guns from their holsters. He cocked both hammers and levelled the .45s at the clerk.

'You telling me that the Gun Master killed my brother?' he asked.

Jones nodded. 'He did. Mr Carey killed your brother up in his room.'

Black looked at his men. 'What kinda showdown happens in a hotel room, boys?'

'The murdering kind, Forrest,' Darren said.

Black stretched his arms and aimed both his guns at the shaking clerk. 'Is that what happened? Did he murder Zane?'

Jones shook his head.

'I don't know,' he nervously stammered as his hands rose above his head. 'The Gun Master seen your brother's name on the register and went upstairs. The next thing I heard was shooting.'

'Where is Rex Carey, boy?'

'I heard that he rode out,' Jones answered.

'Where'd he go?' Black pressed.

'Honest, I don't know where he went.'

A rage overwhelmed Black. His eyes rolled in their sockets as a wave of madness surged through every fibre of his body. He shook his head at the helpless clerk.

'Wrong answer, boy!' Black mercilessly squeezed both triggers. Two lethal shots of red-hot venom spewed from his gun barrels and ripped into the clerk. The dead youngster hit the wall hard, sliding from his chair. A scarlet stain trailed his corpse down to the ground as it limply crashed on to the floor.

With the look of sickening triumph etched on his cruel face, Black turned and glared at his men. He swung around and faced the other terrified guests. They looked at his hollow eyes as he stepped toward them with his smoking six-shooters in his hands.

'Reckon you all seen that, huh?' Black grunted as he cocked both .45s again. As three men and a female tried to dash for the door the laughing Black blasted them. One by one, he watched their dead bodies stumble and fall. 'Never leave any witnesses — my brother told me himself.'

Nervously, Edwards moved to the side of Black as the insane killer shook the spent casings from his guns. 'We come here to rob a bank, Forrest. We don't need trouble with the law.'

Black closed and locked the smoking chambers of his weapons and glared into the eyes of the heavily bandaged Edwards.

'There won't be no trouble from that fat coward who wears the tin star, Bob,' Black said as he marched to the hotel door and stared at the telegraph office. He raised both guns and blasted at the wires leading to and from the small wooden structure. His deadly accurate shots severed each of the wires cleanly. 'Now there won't be any trouble with outsiders either. We got this town in the palm of our hands, boys.'

Monk rubbed his jaw.

'What about the bank, Forrest?' he asked. 'Zane had a plan about how we can rob it but I figure it died with him.'

Black nodded as he watched the smoke trailing from his gun barrels. 'We don't need no plan, boys. We'll just take what we want and kill every witness that could get us neck-stretched.'

'What about the Gun Master, Forrest?' Don Holly asked.

'He rode out before we even got here,' Black said. 'I figure he's a coward just like the sheriff. Rex Carey ain't gonna give us any misery.'

Monk moved to the side of the deadly Black. 'I don't reckon Carey is yella, Forrest. It might be smart if we kept an eye out for that *hombre*.'

'We'll watch out for Carey, but I'm betting he's long gone.' Black screwed up his eyes and stared through the smoke that trailed up from the barrels of his guns at the bank. He began to laugh. 'We'll still rob that damn bank though, boys. Just like brother Zane planned. When I'm finished there won't be a red cent left in Willow Creek.'

Darren bit his lip. 'When do you figure on robbing that bank, Forrest?'

Black eyed his men.

'Right now,' he drawled. 'C'mon.'

The five men led their mounts across the street toward the bank. Black had a wide grin carved into his features as he held his smoking guns in his hands. None of the men who followed Black were smiling. They knew they had to obey him or end up like the pitiful folks in the hotel.

10

For a man of his weight, Will Hume rode well. His hands urged the saddle horse to maintain a pace it had never reached before. The dusty road led to Judge Oliver's cattle spread and the lawman knew that somewhere along its length he might find the tall, handsome rider he was seeking.

The sheriff drove the horse onward through the unrelenting sunshine. A scattering of trees gave some relief from the rays of the merciless sun perched high in the cloudless blue sky as Hume continued to encourage the sturdy mount on toward the distant cattle ranch. Even though he had not ridden a horse for the last eighteen months nobody would have realized it. Hume had lost none of his former skills in the saddle as he steered the animal along the shimmering trail.

Gigantic crimson rocks flanked the lawman as he continued to kick the flanks of his mount.

Over and over again Hume whipped the shoulders of the galloping horse with the tails of his long leathers. The lawman was afraid of what he had left behind him in Willow Creek, but was even more afraid of slowing his pace.

He knew that he had to warn Carey of the potential danger back in town. There was no way he could prevent Black or his cronies from doing their worst, but Hume could warn the famed Gun Master that to return was to invite almost certain death.

The lawman rode on. The saddle horse rode up the trail and rounded a bend at full flight. Then the lawman caught a glimpse of the grey stallion and its elegant master heading toward him.

Hume drew back on his reins. Dust billowed from his horse's hoofs as they dug into the loose sand.

His mount abruptly stopped. A cloud

of choking dust swirled around both horse and rider. As Hume chewed on the dust Carey trotted up to the sweat-soaked sheriff and pulled back on his reins.

'What in tarnation are you doing all the way out here?' Carey asked the panting lawman. 'You don't look like you're built for riding.'

Will Hume gave an exhausted nod of his head.

'I ain't built for riding,' Hume gasped in agreement. He reached out and steadied himself on the saddle horn of the younger horseman. 'I had to come out here and find you, boy.'

Carey frowned. 'What the hell for?'

Sheriff Hume coughed. 'Trouble is brewing in Willow Creek, by my figuring.'

'What kinda trouble?' Carey was curious as he stared at the dishevelled sheriff. 'And how does it concern me?'

Hume leaned closer. 'Black's brother and four other varmints are in town looking for Zane. I bumped into Forrest

Black in the Mustang Saloon. I thought he was gonna kill me where I stood. That critter is loco, and him and his boys are fuelled up with gut-rot whiskey.'

Carey raised his eyebrows. He could not hide his concern at the sheriff's words.

'Forrest Black is in Willow Creek?'

'Yep, he sure is and he brung an army with him.' Hume shook his head helplessly. 'Leastways, they're toting more guns than any troop of soldiers I ever seen.'

The Gun Master considered what the sheriff had told him and then thumbed his jaw. 'Did he say anything to tell you why he came to Willow Creek, Sheriff?'

'He just said that he was here to meet Zane.' Hume breathed heavily. 'I beat me a trail to find you. That critter has the eyes of a crazy man, boy. God only knows what he'll do when he finds out Zane is dead.'

'And I killed him,' Carey added.

'That you did,' Hume agreed.

Every instinct told Carey that he

should ride as far away from Willow Creek as was possible, but an even stronger instinct told him that he could not run. He had killed Zane Black and it was he who had to face Forrest.

'You're scared, Sheriff,' Carey noted. 'I don't blame you.'

'I sure am.'

'Why'd you come to warn me?' Carey asked the sheriff. 'If Black found out that you warned the critter that bettered his brother, he'd be mad as hell.'

'I didn't know what to do,' Hume admitted. 'I never seen a bunch of vermin like them before. I knew that if they got you in their sights they'd destroy you. I couldn't let you ride back into that so I came looking for you. Mainly 'coz I didn't know what else to do.'

Carey patted the lawman's back.

'Don't fret none, Sheriff. If there's trouble in town I reckon it's my fault. If I hadn't killed Zane, his brother wouldn't be itching to get even. I'll have to straighten this out.'

Hume looked stunned. 'You're going back to town?'

'Sure.'

'I figured you'd ride away from Willow Creek as fast as this grey could carry you, boy,' the sheriff said. 'I didn't mean for you to risk your neck facing up to them critters. I came to warn you.'

Rex Carey had not even considered fleeing. He raised an eyebrow and looked hard at the lawman.

'You warned me,' Carey said into the heat haze. 'For that I'm obliged.'

The sheriff straightened up on his saddle. 'Seems to me that all I've done is encourage you to be suicidal. Why ain't you spurring that grey and high-tailing it, boy?'

'Why would I do that?' Carey asked. 'For all we know Forrest Black might not hanker to tangle with me after he knows that I killed his brother.'

Hume shook his head. 'You ain't looked into his eyes. He's crazy, I tell

94

you. He's a crazy critter with a matched pair of guns and a bunch of cohorts to back up his play. You can't even think about heading back into town. If he don't kill you, his men will.'

Carey smiled. 'They might try, but so have a lot of folks over the years. I'm not scared of them or any other gun-toting varmint, Sheriff. It ain't my way to run away. I face my demons head on.'

'You'll die, boy.' Hume sighed.

'We all gotta die sometime.' Carey gathered up his reins and ran a hand along the neck of his grey stallion. 'The thing is I'm not afraid of dying.'

'You oughta be.'

The Gun Master rubbed his sweat-soaked neck and thought for a while before he asked the lawman a question that was troubling him.

'Why do you reckon Forrest and his gang would come to your town?' Carey posed. 'I know his brother was here, but there has to be another reason.'

Hume thought about the question.

'Yeah, that is kinda odd, ain't it? Forrest Black shows up in Willow Creek with a small army. Why?'

'Maybe he needs them,' Carey offered. 'Maybe Forrest didn't come here to visit his brother, but came here to do something. It was rumoured that over the years Zane was the brains behind a lot of bank and train hold-ups, but nothing was ever proven. I've got a feeling that Forrest and his henchmen came here to do what his brother had planned. Something that requires a bunch of well-armed men.'

Sheriff Hume screwed up his face. 'You don't reckon they're here to do some stealing, do you?'

'Is there much money in town?' Carey asked the lawman. 'Maybe a lot more than usual?'

The expression of Hume's wrinkled face changed as something dawned upon him. He nodded.

'There sure is,' he said. 'The bank gets a few shipments of used bank notes from the state treasury every six months or so, boy. They have to incinerate them for the treasury in exchange for new bank notes.'

The Gun Master turned his stallion and stared at the sheriff. 'And the bank has received the old bank notes?'

Hume nodded. 'They've received most of them. They came in last week.'

'When does the bank burn them?'

'Not until they have all of them,' Hume said. 'That shouldn't be for another week or so. Once they get all of the old money they burn them in one batch.'

Carey pulled the brim of his hat down to shield his eyes and then asked one final question.

'How much money do you figure is in the bank right now, Sheriff?'

'I ain't rightly sure but it has to be in the tens of thousands,' Hume guessed. 'I had to stand guard when they unloaded the wagon and locked it up in the bank safe.'

Rex Carey smiled. 'That's why they're here. Zane must have wired his brother telling him that the bank was full of old bank notes that were going to be destroyed. That's why Forrest is here with four hired guns, Sheriff. They're going to rob the bank and fill their saddlebags with a fortune in greenbacks.'

'But how would Zane have known?'

'Zane Black knew a lot of things he shouldn't have known.'

Hume turned his saddle horse. 'Even if you're right, this ain't no reason for you to risk your life and face up to them stinking varmints.'

'You're wrong, Sheriff.' Carey opened his cigar case and chose one of the thin black smokes from within. 'I made it my business when I killed Zane Black. If I'm right about the bank robbery I'll stop them.'

'But you'll have to risk your neck for nothing but old money, son,' Hume said. 'Why bother? Let them steal it and ride.'

Carey shook his head. 'Black never leaves any witnesses, Sheriff. He'll kill every man, woman and child that sees him stealing. That's why he's never been convicted of any of his crimes. No witnesses. That makes it my business.'

Hume watched as the elegant horseman lit his cigar and allowed its smoke to filter from between his teeth. As Carey returned the case to his pocket he spoke.

'Why risk your life, Carey?' Hume repeated. 'You're just one man and there's five of them cut-throats.'

Carey gripped the cigar in his teeth.

'Why? Because I'm the only man in a hundred miles who can stop them, Sheriff. And I intend stopping them one way or another,' Carey said firmly. 'After all, I'm the Gun Master.'

No sooner had the words left his lips when Carey slapped his handsome mount into action. Will Hume watched in awe as the grey stallion obeyed its master and began to gallop through the blazing sunshine back toward Willow Creek.

'And I gotta go back 'coz I'm the

elected sheriff.' Hume sighed and dragged the head of the saddle horse around. 'I still reckon that damn vote was rigged.'

And reluctantly the lawman followed.

11

The streets of Willow Creek had emptied long before the sound of gunfire had resonated along its length from the hotel. For a brief moment the entire settlement had fallen back into an eerie silence. All that could be heard was the haunting melody of spurs ringing out as the five hardened gunfighters turned their sights upon the bank. With their freshly acquired mounts in tow the gunmen started to cross the wide, empty street toward their goal. The eyes of a score of onlookers watched from behind lace-covered windows at the grim sight.

At the head of the five deadly gunmen Forrest Black smiled as smoke drifted from his holstered guns. Although the bank was ripe and ready to be robbed that was not the true reason he walked toward it. He had the scent of fresh killings in his nostrils and, like all men addicted to their various vices, Black wanted to add more to his bloody tally.

The afternoon sun beat down mercilessly upon them, yet they seemed neither to notice nor care. There was only one thought upon all of their collective minds and that was to execute the plan that Zane Black had brought them into town for.

Yet, as they strode toward the bank, none of them knew the real reason why Zane had sent for them. They were utterly oblivious to the fact that within the bank's reinforced walls, a fortune in used bank notes awaited destruction. Somehow Zane Black had learned the truth about the vast sum of cash, but he had died before he could inform his brother.

Within the bank, Marcus Cosmo glanced up from behind his desk and stared through the window into the bright, sunlit street. For a moment he maintained his usual smile but then he saw them. Five heavily armed figures heading toward his bank. A dozen years of banking had taught Cosmo that these were no ordinary customers.

It was obvious.

Murderous intent was carved into the face of each one of them.

The five deadly gunmen purposely led their fresh mounts toward him. A sudden panic overwhelmed the banker. He jumped to his feet and glanced at his tellers and gestured frantically at them.

'Lock the door!' Cosmo screamed over and over again at the two tall men.

The pair of tellers looked at the owner of the bank in bewilderment. They had never seen Cosmo appear so terrified before. Nor had they ever known him close the bank early before.

Cosmo began to realize that the shooting he had heard earlier as it echoed around Willow Creek was no innocent cowboys firing at clouds as they celebrated something trivial. The shots he had heard were a stark omen of what was about to occur within his own bank.

He rushed around his desk.

His fevered mind thought about the small fortune that had been stored within his bank. He glanced at the five men again through the window.

They were still heading his way.

They were getting closer with each pounding beat of his heart. He had to lock the door himself, he thought.

Moving faster than he had done for years, Cosmo ran from the desk to the bank's front doors. He turned the key in the lock and then reached up for the large brass bolt.

He had only just managed to take hold of the bolt when he heard the chilling sound of spurs on the board-walk. Cosmo backed away and looked at the door handle. Sweat trailed down his jowls as the handle turned.

One of the five gunmen was trying to enter, he told himself. As the handle rattled Cosmo felt his heart trying to break free of its confines.

He had never been so afraid.

'What's wrong, Mr Cosmo?' one of

the tellers asked as both men walked around the counter toward their employer.

'It's only just turned noon,' the other added. 'How come you've locked up?'

Cosmo swung around and waved his arms at them. They stopped and looked at their employer as if the older man had lost his reasoning.

It sounded like a thunderclap. The deafening sound of a gunshot was followed by the door lock being blasted from the solid wooden doors. Fragments of metal and wood blasted from the lock and clattered across the floorboards.

Then they heard hefty boots kicking at the door. The wide-eyed bankers stared at the large double doors as they shook under the impact.

Suddenly one of the large doors flew off its hinges and came crashing inward in a cloud of dust. It landed between Cosmo and the five gunmen.

Marcus Cosmo stepped between the tellers.

As the sunlit dust swirled into the

bank Forrest Black entered with one of his smoking six-shooters in his hand. The bank was filled with the sound of spurs as his four men trailed him into the bank.

'Good grief!' Cosmo gasped.

'What's going on, Mr Cosmo?' one of the tellers asked as they all backed up to the counter.

Black came to a halt. His eyes studied the room and located the large safe built into the rear wall. It seemed larger than a town of the size of Willow Creek would ever require. The sinister killer had no idea what it was built to hold. A smile etched his unshaven face as he aimed his gun at the three bank men.

'Open the safe,' Black growled at them.

Cosmo stood between his tellers with his arms raised. 'Who are you? What's all this about?'

Forrest Black lowered his head and inhaled deeply. Without warning he cocked and fired his gun. As the deafening sound of his gunshot echoed around the bank, one of the tellers clutched his chest and looked pathetically at Cosmo.

'I've been shot, Mr Cosmo . . . ' His words faded as the banker watched blood spread across the front of the teller's white shirt.

Before Cosmo could say anything the teller fell on to his knees and then toppled lifelessly forward. The banker blinked hard and then looked at Black.

The devilish Black cocked his gun again.

'Open up that damn safe before I kill you all,' he warned the banker as he blasted another deathly accurate shot into the other teller.

Cosmo stared in horror as the young man at his side buckled and fell on to the floor. A pool of crimson spread out from the dead body.

The banker looked at Black.

'I'll open the safe,' he said.

Forrest Black appeared disappointed. He tilted his head as Darren and Monk trailed the sobbing Cosmo to the huge safe. He watched as the banker slid two brass keys into twin locks and turned them.

Marcus Cosmo gripped a handle and turned it until the safe made a clicking noise. Then he pulled the nine-inch-thick door toward him to reveal the contents of the impressive vault.

'Holy cow!' Darren exclaimed.

Monk looked into the safe and then turned to the others and gestured as he searched for words that would convey his own disbelief.

'Look in this safe,' Monk stammered. 'You ain't ever seen so much money as this old banker got stashed in here.'

Black lowered the smoking six-shooter and strode across the bank and peered within its belly. Even he seemed stunned by the fortune his eyes were looking at.

As the rest of the gang gazed in shock at the piles of cash stacked from floor to ceiling, Black turned and moved closer to Cosmo.

He grabbed the banker by his lapels and hoisted him off the floor. Black looked into Cosmo's eyes.

'What you got that much money for?' he questioned.

Cosmo could not speak. His attention was on his two dead tellers.

Black shook Cosmo again. 'Answer me. How have you got so much money in that safe, old timer?'

Edwards stepped up to Black. 'That must be why Zane sent for you, Forrest.'

Black released his grip on the banker and turned toward Edwards. He considered Edwards's words and then started to smile again.

'That must be right, Bob,' he drawled. 'That's why Zane wanted me to ride all the way here to rob a little bank. A little, small-town bank, full to overflowing with money.'

Cosmo was no longer afraid. He was too shocked by the events of the previous few minutes to be afraid. He wandered across the blood-smeared floor to where his tellers lay. He knelt down and smothered his face with his hands.

Black pushed Edwards aside and then

cocked his gun and aimed it at the kneeling banker. He squeezed his trigger. Cosmo arched and then fell over the bodies.

'Why'd you do that, Forrest?' Edwards asked. 'That fat old man couldn't do us any harm.'

Black looked at the men. 'Find as many bags as you can and fill them with all the larger bills. Nothing smaller than ten-dollar bills. We don't wanna weigh them new nags down.'

Edwards looked at Black as the demented killer shook the spent casings from his gun and then started to reload.

'Why did you kill that pathetic old man?' he asked again.

Black paused and looked at Edwards.

'I told you before, Bob,' he said. 'I never leave anybody alive who could get us hanged.'

Edwards touched his bandaged ear and nodded. He then clawed the air at the other gunmen. 'Come on, boys. Let's rustle up some bags like Forrest said and fill them with as much of this cash as we can handle.'

Forrest Black walked arrogantly across the bloodied floor toward what remained of the bank's door. He stared out into the blinding sunlit street.

'Real quiet, ain't it?' he muttered as his gun slid back into its holster. 'It's funny how quiet a town gets when the shooting starts.'

'How many bags do you reckon we'll need, Forrest?' Holly called out from across the bank. 'We've only managed to find four so far.'

Black tilted his head. His eyes smouldered in their sockets as he watched his gang gathering canvas bags together to fill with the only part of the vast fortune they had discovered.

'On second thoughts, I reckon it would be a sin to leave most of that loot here, boys,' he said, dryly. 'We gotta take it all, just like Zane wanted.'

The men stopped and stared at Black.

Black snapped his fingers at Monk.

'Go get a wagon from someplace, Eli,' he ordered. 'A nice big wagon.'

12

The echoes of gunfire floated across the trail road as Rex Carey drove his mount toward the outskirts of Willow Creek. As the resolute rider reached the first of the town's structures the Gun Master hauled rein and allowed the dust from his stallion's hoofs to settle. The horseman steered his horse to the side of one of the buildings and then swiftly dismounted.

Carey wrapped his long leathers around a wooden upright and then stared down into the heart of the settlement. Had he not known the truth, he might have considered that Willow Creek was a ghost town.

There was no sign of anyone.

From where he stood Carey could see along the length of the main street. His eyes narrowed upon the five mounts tied up outside the bank.

He nodded to himself.

'That must be the bank,' he muttered. The grey stallion nodded and clawed at the dust.

He was about to continue on into Willow Creek when he heard the hoofs of the lawman coming up behind him. Carey turned and watched as Will Hume pulled back on his reins and stopped beside him.

'What do you think you're doing here, Sheriff?' Carey asked the exhausted lawman as his bulky frame slid from the saddle horse and he steadied himself.

Hume looked at the younger man. 'I'm here to help you, son.'

Carey smiled. 'A tuckered-out lawman ain't much help when the going gets tough. Maybe you ought to just stay here and look after our horses.'

The sheriff looked offended. 'Are you telling me that you know this town as well as me, sonny?'

The Gun Master shrugged. 'I reckon not.'

Hume moved closer.

113

'Then I'm gonna help you,' he said firmly.

'If you like ducking bullets then tag along,' Carey invited. 'I ain't got no objections.'

The lawman waved his finger under the taller man's nose.

'I'll tell you something, Carey,' he started. 'You might be real slick with that six-shooter but you don't know every inch of Willow Creek like I do.'

Carey thought about the statement. 'You're right. I reckon a little bit of local knowledge might come in handy if I'm gonna get close to Forrest Black and his henchmen.'

'And you'll need to know more than they do if you're gonna survive in town.' Hume nodded. 'I was here when this town was built. I happen to know it like the back of my hand. You'll need me if you're gonna get close to them critters.'

Carey looked back at the long main street and the multitude of side streets that branched off it. Apart from the long main road there was no sense to it. The Gun Master realized that the stocky lawman might prove invaluable.

'I sure could use help in finding my way through those back streets, Sheriff,' Carey admitted before holding out his hand. 'I'd be proud to tag along with a tuckered-out old lawman.'

Hume laughed and shook the outstretched hand.

'I'll show you how tuckered-out I am,' he said.

Carey looked up at the cloudless sky. He could feel the unrelenting heat of the sun burning his face. He watched as Hume tied his leathers next to where he had secured his own mount.

'Are you ready?' Carey asked.

'I was born ready, sonny,' the sheriff growled. 'You just follow me and you'll not get yourself picked off by them rascals.'

Both men moved away from their horses and headed down toward the sun-bleached array of structures. They stayed close to the buildings. Hume led the way and Carey followed. After only a few dozen yards it became obvious to the Gun Master that Hume did know Willow Creek like the back of his hand. He seemed to know every short cut.

Carey said nothing but was impressed at the speed and agility the sheriff showed as they made good progress through the maze of back streets and alleyways.

The wily lawman led his younger companion through every broken fence and into one back alley after another as they made their way closer and closer to the bank.

'How far is it?' Carey whispered as the pair jumped over an adobe wall.

'Not far, boy,' Hume answered. 'Keep close.'

The lawman ensured that their route to the bank was unseen by those within the sturdy bank. Carey trailed Hume and stayed close to his heels. They moved silently like mountain lions stalking their prey. They were unseen, unheard and determined to catch their unwitting targets off guard.

They pushed out from some bushes and raced across the dusty lane toward a block of structures which had been built so close to one another that there was hardly enough room between them to slide a cigarette paper.

Carey gritted his teeth and stared at the side of the structure in dismay. 'We'll have to go around.'

'No we won't.' The lawman winked as he got down on to his knees.

Carey knelt down beside Hume. He was confused by the knowing grin upon the old-timer's face.

Hume was not discouraged like his young companion for he knew something that the Gun Master did not. Carey edged close to his guide and frowned.

'How are we gonna reach the bank from here, Sheriff?' he wondered as he stared at the seemingly solid obstruction. 'A woodpecker couldn't get through here.'

Hume looked at Carey and tapped the side of his nose.

'Look and learn, boy.' He smiled.

Rex Carey watched as the lawman moved to the base of the building and placed his hands on the boards. The sheriff pressed one side of what seemed like a solid wall and it popped out like a door.

'What in tarnation?' Carey gasped.

'They had to make sure that workmen could get under these buildings, boy,' Hume explained as he started to crawl beneath the structure. 'So they made sure that they were accessible.'

'What for?' Carey asked.

'How else could you paint under them?' Hume sighed as he started into the dark void. 'You sure don't know much about wooden houses, do you? If you don't paint their bellies they rot.'

'I reckon my education is mighty sorrowful,' Carey admitted as he tried to keep up with the lawman. 'So you can move under these buildings all the way to the bank?'

'Close enough, boy,' Hume said. 'Close enough.'

Carey followed the sheriff deeper into the strange underground foundations. Shafts of blazing sunlight filtered through the numerous cracks and gaps in the wooden base of the buildings as both men crawled on their hands and knees under the three structures.

They continued to manoeuvre between the wooden props that ensured the buildings remained where they were. For more than five minutes they carefully moved under the three buildings until they again closed in on another seemingly solid obstruction.

Carey crawled up beside the lawman.

He watched as Hume expertly manipulated the boards. A blinding shaft of sunlight hit them as the utility door swung outward.

Hume was about to move out into the sweltering heat when the hand of his companion stopped him. Hume looked at Carey and was about to speak when he saw the determined expression upon his face.

The Gun Master looked to both sides

and then nodded at the sheriff. They clambered out and rose back to their feet.

'Where are we?' Carey asked Hume.

The sheriff pointed. 'The bank is just beyond that building, son.'

'Can't we crawl under that one as well?' Carey innocently asked the sheriff.

Sheriff Hume frowned at the famed Gun Master. 'Nope, they figured it would be a little tempting to folks, being able to crawl under a bank.'

Carey nodded. 'Reckon that would be a little tempting.'

For the first time since they had started out from the outskirts of town Carey drew his gun and instinctively checked its chambers.

The sheriff stared at the gun and then noticed that Carey only had one holster hanging from his hip. His bushy eyebrows rose.

'You only got one gun?' he asked.

Carey nodded. 'Yep, I just have the one.'

'I'd have thought that someone called

the Gun Master would have more guns.' Hume exhaled.

Carey smiled briefly. 'I only need one.'

13

The handsome female hid behind the window drapes of the café as she stared across at the bank. For more than a half-hour she had been trapped within the empty diner, unable to escape for fear of being noticed by the five ruthless outlaws. Sally Quinn knew that the shots she had heard from the bank had gone unanswered. Her beautiful eyes had searched the street in desperation, but unusually there was no sign of anyone out in the midday sun.

It was as though every one of the citizens of Willow Creek had hidden themselves away within their homes, safely out of sight. She pressed the palm of her hand against the door frame and stared through the glass at the bank and its crippled doors.

Terror gripped at her bosom as she vainly tried to remain calm. A frightening thought kept filling her mind as she kept watch on the bank.

What if one or more of the deadly killers got hungry?

She ran her long, slim fingers through her dark mane of wavy hair and pushed a strand off her face — a face with droplets of sweat across its pretty contours.

For Sally feared that the lingering aroma of food might draw the gang to her modest establishment. Her head swung back as she looked around the small café.

The only way in or out was through the door she was now pressed up against. She swallowed hard.

She knew that there was not one man in town with the courage to help her if the five savage gunmen chose to satisfy their appetites.

A chill engulfed Sally.

What if those appetites strayed from mere food? What if they strayed to . . . more basic hungers?

Sally was a handsome female and she knew it. She had always worked hard and kept herself pure in hope that one day her knight in shining armour might happen to ride into her life.

Now she began to tremble.

She backed away from the door. A table stopped her and she raised her apron to her mouth. A monstrous fear urged her to scream, but she knew that the only ears it would fill were those of the five heavily armed men she had seen enter the bank violently moments before the shooting began.

Sally Quinn hesitated in the centre of the dining area of her café. She continued to stare through the glass pane in the locked front door. Nothing in the street escaped the telling rays of the overhead sun.

What could she do?

She felt sick.

There was nothing she could do, absolutely nothing.

All she could do was wait. Wait for the inevitable.

Then she heard the sound of chains rattling outside as two large horses drew a covered wagon from the livery. Fighting her natural fear, she stepped forward once more.

Sally resumed her place beside the door frame. Her eyes spotted the reflection of the wagon as it was driven toward the five saddle horses tied up at the hitching rail outside the bank.

Then the wagon came into view.

She saw one of the gunmen sitting upon the well-sprung driver's seat. He carefully turned the horses into the alley next to the bank. Eli Monk pushed the brake pole forward with his boot and wrapped the reins around it. As he rose to jump down he stopped and glanced across the sundrenched street at the café. Sally instinctively moved back out of sight, but not quickly enough. Eli Monk's head tilted as he glimpsed the shapely young woman through the glass of the café door.

A cruel smile etched his face as he leapt down and moved back to where the five horses were tethered. He paused by a wooden upright, dragged a match down it and cupped its flame to his cigarette. Smoke drifted from his mouth as he slowly made his way back to the shattered bank doors.

Sally bit on the hem of her raised apron as she stood in the shadows of her small café.

She closed her beautiful eyes and started to sob.

Her worst fear had been realized, she thought. One of the gunmen had seen her.

14

Forrest Black stood beside Holly as Darren and Edwards placed the four canvas bags in the centre of the bank. Each of the sacks was filled with a fortune, yet there was still far more remaining in the large safe. Black heard the spurs ring out as Monk strolled in from the blazing sun across the bloodstained floorboards.

'What took you so long, Eli?' Black snarled as he tapped ash off his cigar and watched it land upon the dead body of Marcus Cosmo. 'You've been gone the best part of half an hour.'

There was a knowing smile on the face of the gunman as he strolled closer to Black and the others. He sucked hard on his cigarette and then dropped its twisted butt into the pool of crimson gore that surrounded the three bankers.

'I had to convince the blacksmith it

was healthier for him if he let me borrow the wagon and two of his prized nags,' Monk said. 'He took a lot of convincing, Forrest.'

Black stared through the smoke that was drifting from his mouth. He moved closer to Monk and then lowered his head. His eyes seemed to burn holes in anything they focused upon.

'How come you smiling, Eli?' Black asked.

Monk rubbed a thumb along his jaw. 'I just saw something that whetted my appetite, Forrest.'

Black glowered at Monk. 'What the hell are you talking about, Eli?'

Monk saw the other three gunmen moving closer to him, yet the memory of the sight he had glimpsed in the café fuelled his smile.

'I just saw a real pretty gal over in the café yonder, Forrest,' he explained. 'I saw her when I jumped down from the wagon after I left it in the alley.'

Black inhaled cigar smoke deeply as he pondered on the statement. He strode across to one of the bank windows and peered past its green drape. The café looked as though it were closed, but a locked door never stopped Black. He pulled the cigar from his mouth and rested his hand on the brass railing set across the window.

Monk was at his side. 'Can you see her?'

'Nope,' Black replied.

'I reckon she's still in there,' Monk said.

'Maybe she is.' Black considered thoughtfully. 'Was she good-looking, Eli? Was she worth crossing the street for?'

Eli Monk rubbed his hands together. 'As pretty as a Georgia peach, Forrest,' he sighed.

'It's bin a long while since I tasted a Georgia peach,' Black said as he placed the cigar to his lips and sucked even more smoke from it.

Monk frowned. 'But I seen her first.'

Black dismissed the gunman. 'So what?'

The others were trying to get a look at the café when Black turned and pointed at the canvas bags. On his face was a cruel look that they each recognized and feared.

'Take that loot to the wagon and empty the cash on to the flatbed. Then come back in here and refill them bags,' Black growled as he glanced over his shoulder through the window. 'You keep going until every last dollar bill has been loaded on to the wagon. Then you lace up the canvas.'

Reluctantly they obeyed. Only Monk remained beside Black as the tall gunman sucked on his cigar thoughtfully.

'What you gonna do, Forrest?' he asked.

Black's demonic eyes darted at Monk. 'I'm gonna get me some vittles over in the café. Any objection?'

Monk followed Black to the doorway like a whipped dog. He was angry that Black was going to do what he had planned on doing.

'Can I come with you, Forrest?'

Black paused on the boardwalk. He looked at Monk. There was an insane fury in his face as he chewed on his cigar.

'You help the boys fill that wagon with cash, Eli.'

'That ain't fair!' Monk raged. 'I seen her first. I ought to get the first crack at her, Forrest.'

Black lowered his hands and rested them on his holstered six-shooters. A terrifying grin bore down on Monk.

'Do as I say or I'll surely kill you, Eli,' Black mumbled as his teeth chewed on the end of his cigar. 'I'm gonna sink my teeth into that Georgia peach yonder and if you're lucky you can have anything that happens to be left when I'm finished.'

There was an insanity in Black that only a fool would fail to recognize. His icy glare frightened even the most courageous of men. It was hard for most people to hide their darker side, and for Forrest Black it was well-nigh impossible. He would kill anyone who dared to defy him, and it showed.

Fearfully, Monk backed away. In all his days Black was the only gunfighter he had never had the guts to draw against. He nodded and walked back into the heart of the bank.

Black's cold stare defied any of his henchmen to stand up against him. As always, none of the four dared to even argue with him.

Black swung on his heels and stepped toward the edge of the boardwalk. He looked across the street at the café. It was impossible to see into it as the bright sunlight reflected off its window and door glass, but his lustful eyes tried. He knew Monk would never lie to him. If Monk said he had spied a female, it was true.

The last of the notorious Black brothers stepped down to the sand and began his approach to the café. It was impossible for him to do anything else. It was as though invisible ropes were pulling him across the sand.

He pulled the cigar from his lips and crushed it in his hand. He dusted the ash and tobacco and continued his walk.

The closer he got, the stronger the scent of cooked food became. Yet there was another aroma which filled his flared nostrils as he reached the café.

It was the even more tempting scent of a female.

'It's bin a long time since I had me a square meal and dessert.' Black drooled at the thought of getting his hands on a female. Any female.

Black was like a ravenous dog as he moved to the locked café door and tried its handle. He inhaled deeply again and caught the natural perfume all females attract men with.

'Eli was right — there is a woman in here,' Black mumbled as he shook the door handle again. He pressed his face up against the glass and squinted into the café. Sally was hiding, but she had made the mistake of passing through the beaded drape at the back.

Forrest Black's eyes focused on the swaying beads.

'I was right,' he grunted as the glass steamed up from his heavy panting. 'I knew I was right.'

Black glanced over his shoulder. The four men were doing exactly as he had instructed them. They were carrying bags filled with used banknotes and scattering them on to the flatbed of the wagon. He focused on the door and stepped back to the edge of the boardwalk.

Every sinew in his menacing frame wanted her now. No door could stop him. His greasy hands ran down the side of his shirt as he steadied himself. Then, like a rattler, he jolted into action.

He kicked the door powerfully. His boot hit the lock squarely. Wood and glass shattered across the café floor. He moved into the small room and glared lustfully at the curtain as its strings of beads swung back and forth.

'I know you're in there, girl!' Black growled. 'I can smell you.'

A cloud of dust fell like snow all around the deadly gunman. He grabbed a chair and flung it aside. Nothing was going to stop him now. He no longer had any other thought in his mind. Every consideration had been washed away in the flood of lustful yearnings which burned like branding irons inside his loins.

Unable to control herself, Sally gave out a pitiful scream. The gunman smiled.

'I'm coming, girl,' he sneered. 'If you're good to old Forrest I'll let you live after I've pleasured you.'

Unable to subdue her terror, Sally screamed again from inside the small kitchen. With the bright sunshine behind Black it was like watching a strange animal lumbering toward her.

Black crushed the debris underfoot as he walked across the café. The aroma of a dozen cooked meals still lingered, yet it was not the food he craved.

It was her.

Only she could satisfy his hunger.

Sally had moved as far back into the kitchen as she could, but it was useless. There was no escape and she knew it.

She could hear the terrifying spurs that rang out with every step he took on his advance toward her.

Desperately, Sally looked around for anything to protect herself with. Her eyes fixed upon a carving knife in the sink. She grabbed it. Her shaking hand held the gleaming weapon at arm's length but she knew that when men were roused even a razor-sharp knife could do little to dampen their lust.

Sally could see the ominous Black through the swaying beaded drape. He was moving closer. To the innocent female it was like watching her own executioner approach. For the first time in her short life she knew what it was like to face someone who had death oozing from every pore of his dishevelled form.

'Ain't worth your while trying to hide, girl,' Black said as he pushed tables and chairs out of his path. 'There's nothing you can do but submit. I'm hungry and you're on the menu.'

Frantically, Sally looked around the kitchen for other weapons that might stop the creature that advanced toward her. She grabbed a skillet and threw it with all her strength at him. It passed through the beaded drape and caught Black on the arm.

He momentarily stopped and rubbed his arm.

'That was a good shot, girl,' he taunted. 'Trouble is, I like my females feisty.'

Undeterred, Black started to walk once more toward the swaying beads. She could see his face now. It was dark but it was not dirt that stained his features, but pure evil. Sally tried to remain courageous but then, as she held the knife in her shaking hand, she saw his eyes.

Sally had never seen eyes like his before.

They seemed to glow as he parted the beads and moved into the unlit kitchen. It was like looking into the eyes of the Devil himself, she thought.

There was a crazed expression carved into his face.

Had this hideous creature crawled

from the bowels of Hell in search of fresh, innocent victims? Panic gripped Sally as the true gravity of her situation dawned upon her.

This man was not just going to assault her, she realized. He was going to do unimaginable things to her and then, if she was lucky, he would leave her broken body alive. She would be shunned. Branded as being little better than a harlot.

Fear of the unknown overwhelmed Sally.

Black grinned at her. Even the knife did not seem to scare him as she waved its honed blade at him.

'Stay back, mister!' Sally warned. 'I'll surely kill you if you keep coming.'

Black stopped and looked straight at her. He smiled. It was the smile of death and Sally knew nothing could stop him.

'You ain't gonna kill me, girl,' he said. 'You ain't the sort to kill anything.'

Sally knew he was right but prayed for the strength to prove him wrong. Her beautiful eyes darted over every inch of the drooling man with the expensive gunbelt and two pearl-handled gun grips poking out of their holsters. He was covered in trail dust and sweat and each time he spoke the scent of stale whiskey filled the confined space.

'Put that knife down!' he ordered.

'I ain't afraid to use this,' Sally shouted as she swung the knife back and forth. 'You better turn around and walk off, or they'll carry you out of here in a box.'

Black stared at her.

Drool ran from the corners of his mouth as he studied her succulent form.

'I'm gonna give you five seconds to drop that knife, girl,' he warned as he rested a hand on one of his gun grips. 'Then I'll shoot you dead.'

His words stunned her.

Sally inhaled deeply. 'Shoot me . . . dead?'

He nodded. 'Yep, I'll kill you. It don't matter to me if you're alive or dead. I'm still gonna have my way with you. Savvy?'

His words thundered through her.

She did not realize it, but the knife had slipped from her hand and embedded itself into the floorboards at her feet. Sally's eyes widened. She had no experience with any man let alone one like Forrest Black.

'Please don't hurt me, mister,' she begged as he loomed over her.

Forrest Black touched her hair. 'About time you showed some sense.'

She recoiled. 'What do you mean?'

'You've accepted your fate, girl.' The fumes of hard liquor enveloped her. Sally Quinn watched him start toward her. Within a mere heartbeat he had grabbed her. Her small hands beat at his chest and face, but Black did not feel any of her blows. He forced her hands behind her back and buried his filthy face into her neck.

The naïve female had no idea what was happening. She only knew that it repelled her every instinct. Yet no matter how hard she tried to struggle, he had her firmly under his superior strength.

She wanted to scream but could not. Her eyes watched the beaded drapes swinging like the pendulum of a clock. She felt sick.

This was not how it was meant to be.

A thousand thoughts flashed through her terrified mind, but the most glaring was the recent memory of the young stranger who had entered her café that very day. To her shame and regret she recalled how she had treated him so coldly when she discovered his identity. As the greasy hands of Forrest Black crawled over her body like sidewinders, she wished they were those of the Gun Master instead.

If only she had not shunned the handsome youngster he might have stayed and been able to fend off the deadly gunmen and their loathsome leader.

Abruptly, Sally was dragged from her confused dreams by the unrelenting hands and body of the stinking creature now intent on having his way with her.

The weaker she became, the stronger Black grew. He was all over her. Shame filled the young woman as it became obvious that he would not quit until he had gotten what he was intent on getting.

Sally tried to fend Black off, but it was too late.

No matter how much she fought, his brutal strength kept her pinned against the kitchen wall. His face buried itself into her neck while his hand tore her apron from her waist and cast it away.

'Stop!' Sally sighed as her strength and resolve ebbed.

The smell of hard liquor smothered her like a putrid gas, but she was unable to escape his advances. She tried to knee him, but he was far too experienced. He pressed himself hard against her, making it impossible for her to defend herself.

This was not the first time he had done this, she thought. She was not the first victim of his unwanted advances, and would not be the last. Using his weight to hold her in check, Black forced her into a corner as his fingers tore at the fastenings of her dress.

'Stop!' Sally pitifully begged again. 'For heaven's sake, please stop!'

He paused for a moment. His eyes burned into her.

'I like it when a girl begs,' he grunted. 'You keep begging and I'll keep ripping the clothes off your back.'

'Please stop!'

Her cry for mercy fell on deaf ears.

Sally tossed her head back. Her long wavy hair spread across her shoulders as she looked at her attacker. Then she felt his free hand tear at the sturdy fabric of her dress and heard buttons hitting the floor.

'What you doing?'

Her question was immediately answered. His hands had found her flesh. Instantly, she was sickened by the feeling of his searching fingers.

'No! Please, no!' she cried.

Black reached up to her throat and curled his fingers around her frilly lace collar. He gripped it firmly and gritted his teeth in preparation of what he intended to do next. She pulled an arm free and clawed at his face.

Somehow Black seemed even more excited by her act of self-defence. A horrific look filled his features as blood trickled down from three scratches on his face. Sally wriggled and then slapped him as hard as she could. His head rocked on his muscular neck.

Instantly his expression altered from one of desire to one of anger. He forced his face into hers. A fury swelled up inside him.

His eyes narrowed as they burned into her.

'I'm gonna kill you now, bitch,' Black snarled as his ruthless hands slapped her violently over and over again. 'I'll teach you it don't pay to reject Forrest Black. It don't pay at all.'

His furious words had barely left his lips when a shot rang out from somewhere in the street. It echoed around the small café.

Black was both surprised and stunned. He released her and swung on his boot leather as his hands went for his guns. He hauled both weapons free of his holsters and dragged their hammers back until they locked.

His attention was returned to his four cohorts loading up the wagon with the bank's money.

Only half-conscious, Sally slumped and looked at the startled gunman through the locks of her long hair. She watched the gruesome creature rush away from her through the beaded drape. The sound of his spurs marked his every step. Sally fell to the floor and watched droplets of blood fall on to her lap from her nose.

Black stopped by the doorway with his guns in his hands. His eyes darted around the wide street before they focused on the activity directly opposite him.

Darren and Monk were crouched in front of the bank as Edwards staggered out of the alley clutching his chest with both hands.

'What the hell's going on, Bob?' Black yelled.

There was no reply. Edwards somehow managed to look at the gunman and then twisted and fell. Black's ruthless eyes darted around the bright street in search of the mysterious gunman. He held his cocked guns at hip height and then started to walk across the wide street.

His shadow was long and stretched across the lifeless body of Edwards. As Black reached the body he paused for a mere second to stare down upon it.

Still gripping his unfired .45 in his hand, Edwards lay prostrate with a single bullet-hole in his shirt. A crimson hue surrounded the deadly accurate hole. Black knew that whoever had fired the fatal bullet had to be a marksman.

'Is Bob dead, Forrest?' Don Holly called out from just inside the bank doorway.

'He's dead all right,' Black spat.

He continued on toward the bank. His eyes vainly moved to every possible place where he imagined the unknown gunman might be hiding.

Black reached the bank, pushed the five saddle horses aside and stepped up on to the boardwalk. Holly leaned over Black's shoulder.

'We were loading the wagon with cash like you told us, Forrest,' he stammered. 'Me, Slim and Eli was walking back to refill the sacks when we heard the shot in the alley. Some *hombre* must have plugged poor Bob before he even had a chance to fire his gun.'

'Did you see anyone?' Black asked.

Monk and Darren moved nervously back to the relative safety of the bank's doorway.

'We never seen or heard nothing until that shot rang out, Forrest,' Monk said as he held on to his guns. 'Who do you figure it is?'

'Reckon it's the sheriff?' Darren wondered.

Black inhaled deeply. 'The sheriff didn't kill Bob. We met that fat old critter and he was so scared just talking to me I thought he was gonna swoon.'

'Then who?' Holly probed.

'Every grown man in this town high-tailed it as soon as we rode in, Forrest,' Monk added as he looked at the furious Black. 'Who in tarnation would have the guts to go up against us?'

'The Gun Master — who else?' Black growled. 'The same critter that killed my brother Zane must have crawled back into town to finish the rest of us, by my reckoning.'

'The Gun Master!' Darren nervously repeated the name and shook his head fearfully. 'I heard that he's the fastest gun alive.'

'He bested Zane,' Monk stammered. 'He must be fast.'

Black looked all around them. 'I figure he's a back-shooter. He must be to get the better of Bob and Zane.'

Monk looked at Black. 'But they was both shot in the chest, Forrest.'

'Rex Carey tricked them somehow,' Black spat.

Darren rubbed the sweat from his face along his sleeve as he gripped on to his guns.

'Who in tarnation is the critter, anyway?' he asked. 'I never heard of him.'

Holly kept looking around them. 'Whoever he is, he's sure darn dangerous.'

Black pointed his guns in both directions. 'Listen up. I want you boys to go each side and make your way around to the back of the bank. That's where he is. He's hiding like a rat around the back of this bank. When you find him, fill his stinking carcass with lead. Savvy?'

Darren bit his lip. 'You want us to circle the bank?'

'Yep.' Black nodded.

'But he's out there waiting to add notches to his gun.'

Black moved closer.

'You scared of a back-shooter, Slim?'

Darren glanced across at the lifeless body in the street and nodded.

'If I end up like Bob did, then I'm mighty scared, Forrest,' Darren admitted. 'Bob was faster with his .45 than me and look at his pitiful body.'

Black looked at Holly and Monk. 'You go that way. Me and Slim are going down the alley.'

Darren was scared of facing the legendary Gun Master, but he was even more frightened of disobeying Black. He shuffled his feet and cocked the hammers on his guns. He reluctantly trailed Black to the edge of the alley when the scent of smoke filled both their nostrils.

'What the hell's burning, Forrest?' he asked.

Black tilted his head and peered around the corner of the bank. To his horror he saw the wagon ablaze. Burning bank notes rose into the air from the flatbed of the wagon as it was engulfed in flames.

'Our money's burning, Slim,' Black snarled.

15

Sheriff Will Hume was panting like a hound as he took refuge behind the outhouse at the rear of the bank. A knowing smirk filled his features as he looked at the box of matches in his hand before poking it back into his vest pocket. He had done exactly as Rex Carey had instructed him and, even though it pained him to see so much money going up in smoke, he knew that it would cause even more distress to Black and his followers.

The putrid taste of smoke filled his mouth as the lawman cast his attention upon the surrounding area. There were a score of places where someone like Carey could conceal himself, he thought. The fearless Gun Master had already faced down one of Black's best gunmen with deadly accuracy matched with an equal dose of guts.

The sheriff had never seen anyone like Carey. The tall young Gun Master had faced Edwards and beaten him to the draw with a speed that defied belief. Then he had ordered Hume to set fire to the used bank notes and run for cover.

Hume coughed and then peeked out from behind the fragrant privy to the raging fire he had started. The entire wagon was engulfed in blazing fury. Its flames were like devilish arms stretching up at the cloudless heavens whilst black smoke filled the entire area.

The lawman knew that he had done a good job. It would be a while before any of Black's gang could venture down the alley in search of the culprit, he thought.

The air was full of blackened scraps of paper. That was all that remained of the fortune in bank-notes. The heat of the bonfire made them dance all about his exhausted form. He looked behind him at the pair of sturdy horses Carey had released from their traces before he had told him to set fire to the mountain of money stacked on the wagon's flat bed. Both horses kept moving in a vain bid to escape the toxic smoke.

Hume pulled his gun from its holster and held it at his side. His sore eyes vainly searched for the young man he had led to this place. As smoke billowed across the back of the bank and its adjacent buildings, there was no sign of the Gun Master.

Wherever Rex Carey was, the veteran lawman prayed that luck would remain with him. For some strange reason Hume trusted Carey more than he had ever trusted anyone before.

As he considered why this should be he heard running to his right. Hume screwed up his baggy eyes and looked to where the sound of spurs resounded.

The clouds of black smoke eased for a fraction of a heartbeat and allowed the lawman to catch a brief glimpse of the two men who had just rounded the back of the bank. The lawman clutched on to his six-shooter as he pressed his well-rounded belly up against the wooden outhouse.

With their entire arsenal in their hands Don Holly and Eli Monk stopped and surveyed the area. They looked into the black smoke as it twisted and turned around them. Hume moved around the small wooden outhouse and pressed his sweat-soaked spine against it.

He pulled back on his gun hammer and raised his hand. To his horror the two outlaws started to talk.

'Did you hear that, Don?'

'I sure did,' Holly coughed. 'That was a gun hammer.'

'It must be the Gun Master,' Monk stammered.

'Let's find him and kill that varmint.' Holly began to walk toward the outhouse as black clouds of smoke continued to mask both his and Monk's vision.

The sound of their spurs grew louder as both of the hired gunmen slowly walked around the desolate area in search of the man who had gunned down Bob Edwards.

Hume closed his eyes. Sweat rolled down his face as he stood facing the unyielding sun. The tinder-dry wood of the wagon was cracking as the fire burned through its boards, yet the wily old lawman could still hear their spurs.

He swallowed hard and looked around the privy.

For a moment all he could see was black smoke and a million red embers floating within its heart. Then he saw both Monk and Holly. Terror gripped the lawman as he caught momentary glimpses of the hardened gunmen.

Their spurs grew louder.

As the sheriff tried to aim his gun through the clouds of blinding smoke, they saw him.

'There he is, Don!' Monk yelled as he raised both his weapons. 'Behind that privy.'

Even before Hume had time to duck back behind the outhouse both of the gunmen started to blast their guns. Their shots carved through the frail wooden structure. Hume fell to the ground as bullets ripped massive holes in the wooden walls.

As rods of hot lead passed all around him the lawman had to lay face-first in the dirt. Sawdust showered over the sheriff as both Monk and Holly kept blasting their hog legs.

Then suddenly Hume heard a familiar voice interrupt the shooting. Both gunmen ceased their firing and turned to where they could see the lone figure emerge from out of the clouds of black smoke.

Rex Carey stood like a statue. He held his right hand a few inches over his holstered .45 and watched them as they turned to face him.

Monk gritted his teeth. 'That's the Gun Master.'

'But he was just behind the out-house.'

'He ain't there now, is he?'

'Then let's kill the varmint,' yelled Holly.

Both raised their guns and aimed at Carey as he was totally engulfed by the choking cloud of smoke. Even though they were now unable to see their target, Holly and Monk blasted into the smoke.

Suddenly two single shots were returned. Hot tapers of white lightning carved through the smoke and hit their targets.

Monk flew off his feet as Holly buckled.

Will Hume rolled on to his side and looked hard into the smoke as both Holly and Monk hit the ground. They did not move as Rex Carey stepped out of the smoke and stared at the dead bodies.

There was no sign of emotion in his face. He carefully plucked the two spent casings from his gun and replaced them with bullets from his belt.

'Keep your head down, Sheriff,' Casey advised. 'This ain't over yet.'

The lawman scrambled to his knees and was about to speak when he noticed the Gun Master had once again vanished back into the choking smoke.

He rested a hand on the bullet-scarred outhouse.

'Where'd he go?' he asked himself.

It was a question that would soon be answered.

16

The chilling sound of vicious gunfire echoed all around Willow Creek and the last two members of the Black gang still breathed. Both Black and Darren listened to the fading memories of the brief but deadly encounter, and waited for the heat of the wagon to subside and allow them to head down the alley. Neither gunman spoke as a chilling silence enveloped the front of the bank.

Forrest Black rubbed the cold steel of his gun barrel across his cheek as he stared into the smoke-filled alley. He turned and exhaled.

'How come the shooting stopped, Forrest?' Darren asked as he moved from beside the five saddle horses. 'Do you figure Eli and Don got the varmint?'

Something told Black exactly why the shooting had ended and it burned into his craw. The trouble was he could not admit the truth, not even to himself. He remained silent and indicated for his nervous companion to follow him. Darren jumped down into the alley dust and trailed Black.

The two men clutched their weaponry and moved quickly toward the wagon. The burning vehicle was little more than a memory as flames continued to consume the last of its wooden structure. Only its metal hoops remained amid the ashes. The smoke still curled like a demonic genie as they made their way toward it and the rear of the bank.

The heat filled the narrow confines of the alley as both men carefully negotiated a path around the remnants of the smouldering wagon.

'Why are we going to the rear of the bank, Forrest?' Darren asked fearfully as trailed his single-minded leader. 'Are we going to find Eli and Don?'

Black squinted and paused. The black smoke choked his lungs and burned his eyes as they searched for their two cohorts.

Darren reached the shoulder of his

leader. His eyes were like those of a scared rabbit as they darted all around the blackened area.

'Where are they?' he asked.

Black pointed one of his guns straight ahead. 'Yonder.'

Darren stepped forward. His heart pounded like an Apache war-drum as he realized what Black was pointing at. He looked at the two bodies stretched out on the sand.

'Is that Eli and Don?'

Black moved beside him. 'Yep, that's them, Slim.'

'We gotta get out of this town, Forrest,' Darren urged his snarling companion. 'It's cursed!'

Black looked at Darren. His eyes narrowed as he gritted his teeth.

'You make one move for our horses and you'll end up as dead as Eli and Don,' Black spat. 'You stick with me or they'll be digging a hole for you as well.'

Slim Darren gave a nod. 'Anything you say, Forrest.'

'C'mon!' Black forged on through the

dense smoke until they reached the back of the bank. He made no attempt to go anywhere near his two dead men. 'The varmint must be around here someplace, Slim. Keep them eyes peeled. Savvy?'

'I hear you.' Darren stayed glued to Black's broad shoulder. 'Did the Gun Master do this?'

'Yep,' Black snarled as they reached the far corner and began their way back to the main street. 'That bastard has killed four of our boys including Zane, Slim. We gotta fill him with lead before he does any more killing.'

'When we kill that galoot we can get the last of the money from the bank,' Darren said. 'There's still a couple of bags left in that big old safe.'

Black nodded. 'That sure is good to know. Leastways that loco Gun Master didn't burn it all.'

Darren turned around as they made their way back to the front of the large building. If the legendary Gun Master was anywhere close he was determined to see him.

162

As the pair of gunmen reached the main thoroughfare a strange sound filled the air. Black and Darren stopped on the corner of the bank as their five horses moved away from the hitching rail. A shot rang out and echoed around the wide street.

The horses came racing toward them. Darren was about to try and stop the wide-eyed animals when Black grabbed his shoulder and hauled him back.

'The horses are getting away, Forrest!' Darren protested.

'Look!' Black snarled as he pointed one of his six-shooters along the length of the boardwalk.

As the hoof dust cleared, Darren looked and saw the tall Rex Carey standing in the middle of the street. He had his coat-tail pushed over the holstered gun grip and he lingered defiantly, watching both gunmen as they stood behind the corner of the bank.

'Is that him?' Darren asked. 'Is that the Gun Master?'

Black felt his fiery temper rise. 'That's him, OK.'

'He don't look dangerous,' Darren noted.

Black rested an elbow on the wall and glared at the man who had killed so many of his fellow henchmen as well as his own brother.

'Reckon looks can be a tad deceptive, Slim,' the gang-leader growled. 'But I kinda think you're right. He don't look too dangerous, does he?'

'Then why don't we kill him?' Darren suggested as he raised his gun and took aim. 'We could end his misery from here, right now.'

Forrest Black pushed the barrel of his henchman's gun down as he stretched up to his full height. He glanced at Darren.

'Don't waste your lead. Carey's smart,' Black explained. 'He's standing just out of range of our .45s. That critter knows that we'd need a rifle to pick him off at this distance and our Winchesters are on the backs of the horses he spooked.'

'If we run to the hitching rail we'd be close enough to kill him, Forrest.' Darren eyed the Gun Master as he stood in the middle of the sun-baked street.

Black shook his head. 'And he'd kill us before we even got there.'

A cold sweat traced Darren's spine. 'What'll we do?'

'There's only one thing we can do to oblige the back-shooting varmint.' Black slid his guns into their holsters and straightened up to his full height. He led his companion away from the edge of the bank out into the street.

'There is?'

'Yep, there is.' Black pulled a cigar from his vest and bit off its tip. 'Reckon he wants a showdown.'

Darren gulped. 'I don't hanker to trade lead with the Gun Master, Forrest.'

Black leaned over his cohort, threateningly. 'You either stand by me and draw down on that critter, or I'll kill you where you stand, Slim.'

Darren knew that Black never made idle threats. He forced a nervous grin and nodded as they walked into the centre of the street. Their spurs rang out in the afternoon air like the tolling of ominous bells.

'I'm ready to kill that fella when you tell me to,' Darren croaked, nervously.

They reached the middle of the street and stopped. Both gunmen stared at the distant silhouette.

Rex Carey watched as Black struck a match and arrogantly cupped its flame to his cigar. The deadly killer sucked in a lungful of smoke and tossed the match into the dust before casting his murderous attention down the long street at the watchful Carey.

'You know why Carey seems so brave, Slim?' Black mumbled.

'Why, Forrest?' Darren asked as he rubbed his sleeve across his bone-dry mouth.

'The Gun Master happens to think he's the fastest gun around,' Black said as smoke trailed from his mouth.

'Ain't he?' Darren asked.

'Nope,' Black replied. 'I am.'

Black gripped the cigar in his teeth and tapped his cohort on the shoulder. Both men rested their hands on the grips of their guns in readiness. They then started the slow walk toward Rex Carey.

'How will we know when we're in range, Forrest?' Darren gulped as he paced beside Black.

'When I draw we'll be in range,' Black said. 'Just wait 'til I draw and then you slap leather and start shooting.'

Nervously, Darren nodded.

'I sure hope you don't wait too long to draw, Forrest.'

Rex Carey stood his ground. He remained on the exact spot he had chosen to fight the last of the ruthless killers. Unlike his adversaries, Carey had carefully positioned himself so that the mid-afternoon sun was on his back. It was an old trick, but they had fallen for it.

He watched as both men slowly strode toward him.

A bead of sweat trickled down from his hatband and followed the chiselled line of his jaw. If there was any fear in the man known as the Gun Master, it did not show.

Carey waited.

Just like Forrest Black he knew the distance between them was vitally important. He had seen many gunmen misjudge the range of their weaponry over the years. Too far away and bullets fell short of their target. Too close and they ripped through you.

His right hand hovered over his holstered gun. His fingers flexed as though they were playing a piano. Carey lowered his head and stared from under his hat brim at the two merciless killers.

There was no emotion in the Gun Master.

No lust for revenge or an appetite to kill.

He faced them because they had killed far too many innocents in Willow Creek and would kill countless others unless they were stopped. They had to be prevented from killing any more defenceless folks and Carey knew that he was the only person capable of doing just that.

He watched them like an eagle surveys its prey. His eyes did not blink as they fixed on the pair of lethal gunmen. They would not stray from his adversaries until this was over.

Black and Darren stopped.

Rex Carey knew that both men were now in range. He inhaled deeply and watched as Black spat his cigar at the sand between them.

'So, you're the famous Gun Master?' Black shouted before laughing.

'That's what they call me,' Carey said, without moving a muscle.

The fury returned to Black. He pointed an accusing finger and jabbed at the air. 'You killed my brother and you killed most of my boys.'

'And I'll kill you as well, *amigo*,' Carey answered.

'You'll die trying,' Black snarled venomously and went for his guns.

Darren drew both his own .45s when he saw Black make his move.

The street rocked as their hammers sent shafts of lead through rings of gunsmoke at the solitary figure.

Carey snatched his gun from his holster, cocked and fired it. Four shots passed so close to the Gun Master that he could feel their heat.

At a speed most men would have thought impossible, Carey continued to cock and fire his trusty six-shooter at both his attackers.

As choking smoke filled the distance between them, Carey moved to his side, fell to his knees and continued to cock and fire.

Darren fell backwards, clutching his guns in his lifeless hands, but Black was not so easy to kill. Carey knew that he had hit Black with all four of the bullets he had fired at the crazed gunman, but still Black stood, defiantly holding his smoking guns and firing. The only indication that Carey had not missed Black soon became evident. Crimson circles of blood were dotted over the snarling gunman's torso as he trained his guns on Carey.

'Now you're gonna die, Carey,' Black screamed and rushed forward. 'Die like the dog you are.'

Carey pulled on his trigger and heard the sickening sound of a click. His eyes looked at the smoking weapon in his hand and then back at the wounded man who was staggering toward him.

Black laughed.

'Out of bullets, Carey?' he taunted his helpless target.

The Gun Master gave a nod. 'I reckon so, Black.'

The gunman levelled his guns at the kneeling Carey and pulled back on their hammers. His fingers teased the triggers as he revelled in the fact that he had the famed Gun Master at his mercy.

'This is for my brother Zane,' Black hissed.

The sound of deafening gunshots rang out.

17

Finale

The two bullets had erupted from the barrels of Black's guns and hit the ground to either side of Rex Carey. As the Gun Master looked up at his foe, he realized that his expression had altered drastically. There was a look of surprised horror on the face of Forrest Black. It had replaced the triumphant grin that had borne down upon him until only seconds before.

Carey got to his feet and stared at Black. He was totally bemused.

'Black?'

The guns fell from the hands of Black. Then the devilish gunman looked at Carey before he fell to his knees. Only then did Carey notice the carving knife buried deep into the back of the remorseless Black.

The Gun Master watched as Black fell forward. Yet even skewered by the foot-long length of honed steel and riddled with bullets, the gunman still clung to life.

Black gestured to Carey, who leaned over. 'What do you want, Black? You're as good as dead so I reckon you must want to get something off your chest. What is it?'

A laugh came from the prostrate figure.

'I ain't sorry for nothing, Carey!' Black spat as dark blood trickled from the corners of his mouth.

Carey raised an eyebrow. 'Then what do you want?'

A pitiful look came from the wounded outlaw. He stared into the face of the Gun Master.

'Why'd you burn all that money?' he asked. 'That was wrong.'

A strange rattling noise came from within the gunman as the last ebb of life left his physical form. Rex Carey stood up and slid his gun into its holster.

The sight of the knife protruding from the back of the man at his feet confused Carey. Whoever had thrown it had surely saved his life, he thought. He owed somebody in Willow Creek a debt. Still confused, he bit his lip and rubbed the back of his neck. Then a movement from across the street caught his attention. His eyes looked up.

He saw the young woman in the doorway of the café. She was bruised and barely able to stand.

'Sally,' he said.

As Carey ran toward her he remembered how she had seemed troubled by the knowledge that he was known as the Gun Master and lived by his prowess with his gun.

He jumped up on to the boardwalk just as Sally swooned. He caught her in his powerful arms and helped her inside the café and eased her on to a chair close by in the corner.

Carey studied the wrecked café.

Wood and glass were scattered across the floor and the door was barely clinging to its hinges. He knelt beside Sally and took her hand.

'What happened in here?' he asked.

Sally brushed the long strands of her hair off her face and trembled as she spoke. 'That evil critter kicked my door in and tried to . . . '

Carey took in her bruises and her ripped dress, and placed his fingers against her lips.

'Sssshhhh!' he urged. 'I understand.'

'He didn't manage to get the better of me, Rex,' she said. 'Honest. He tried, but he failed. You gotta believe me — he failed.'

Carey looked at her bruised face.

'I know. I can tell by your face that he hurt you, but you're still a mighty handsome lady.'

Sally wiped the tears from her face. She was still shaking as she thought about the horrific ordeal she had gone through during Black's sordid attack upon her. Then she recalled throwing her carving knife at him when he was poised to shoot the man kneeling beside her. Her fingers touched his cheek.

'Are you OK, Rex?' she asked. 'Did he hurt you?'

'I'm fine, Sally.'

She nodded. 'Thank the Lord.'

'Did you throw that knife, Sally?' he asked her.

She raised her head and looked at him. 'Yes, I killed him. After what he done and was intending to do I threw the knife, and I'm glad.'

She began to sob. He comforted her.

'You didn't kill him. I reckon the four bullets I shot him with did the real harm, Sally,' Carey said. 'Your knife just made him miss with his guns. You didn't kill anyone — you saved my life.'

Sally looked up with tears in her eyes. 'I saved your life?'

He nodded and touched her cheek.

'You did, Sally.' He smiled. 'I'm much obliged. It's the only one I've got.'

Both looked up when they heard footsteps outside the café. Sheriff Will Hume stood by the door frame and stared at the damage. Then his eyes drifted across to the female and the Gun Master.

'Don't you go fretting, Miss Sally,' Hume said. 'I'll round up a few boys and we'll straighten this mess up for you in no time. It'll look as good as new by nightfall.'

'Thank you, Will.' Sally nodded.

The sheriff rested his wrists on his hips. 'You must have nine lives, Carey. We're all grateful for what you did though, boy.'

'I had a little help out there, Sheriff,' Carey admitted.

'I told you that one gun ain't enough in your line of work.' Hume grinned.

Rex Carey glanced at the lawman.

'I'll help you clean this place up.' He nodded. 'I owe this little lady my life.'

'You're staying?' Hume asked.

Sally looked at the Gun Master. 'Are you?'

Rex Carey shrugged.

'For a while.'

Suddenly, Sally saw something in Carey's smiling face that she had long thought was impossible — she saw her knight in shining armour.

'How long is 'a while', Rex?' she asked.

He thought for a moment and then his fingers touched her long, wavy, dark hair. 'I'll go when every one of these hairs is as white as snow, Sally.'

She clasped her hands together and stared at them. Sally looked as though she was praying, but there was no need. All her prayers had been answered.

We do hope that you have enjoyed reading this large print book.

Did you know that all of our titles are available for purchase?

We publish a wide range of high quality large print books including:
Romances, Mysteries, Classics
General Fiction
Non Fiction and Westerns

Special interest titles available in large print are:
The Little Oxford Dictionary
Music Book, Song Book
Hymn Book, Service Book

Also available from us courtesy of Oxford University Press:
Young Readers' Dictionary
(large print edition)
Young Readers' Thesaurus
(large print edition)

For further information or a free brochure, please contact us at:
Ulverscroft Large Print Books Ltd.,
The Green, Bradgate Road, Anstey,
Leicester, LE7 7FU, England.
Tel: (00 44) **0116 236 4325**
Fax: (00 44) **0116 234 0205**

Other titles in the
Linford Western Library:

REAPER

Lee Clinton

The Indian Territory is a hellhole of lawlessness. Deputies are gunned down in cold blood, and outlaws are trading arms to renegades. In desperation, a bold and secret plan is designed by two senior US marshals — recruit a new and unknown deputy, who can operate independently to hunt down and kill three notorious outlaws in reprisal. But has the right man been selected? Walter Garfield's background seems more than a little shady, and he appears to have his own agenda . . .

TEXAS VENGEANCE

Ralph Hayes

Luther Bastian's younger brother was murdered by outlaws. Now Bastian is a bounty hunter who comes to kill — unable to be reasoned with, persuaded or bribed. So when a gang of lawless men brutally slay a Texas Ranger, Captain Mallory knows just the man to call on. But during the pursuit, Bastian is befriended by a young woman and a small boy. Can they change his view on the world, and put an end to his quest for vengeance?

SADDLER'S RUN

Harriet Cade

Ben Saddler, sometime soldier of the Confederate Army, has had many jobs: scout, gambler, barkeep, deputy sheriff, road agent, cowboy . . . Now he is a whiskey runner trying to scrape a living in the Indian Territories. His life takes an unexpected turn when he suddenly finds himself responsible for a young girl. Somehow, he must escort her to safety; evade capture by the law; outgun those who would kill him; and negotiate his way through an Indian uprising. Can he succeed?

LONG SHADOWS

Clyde Barker

For many years, Colonel Robert Farrance has lived a respectable life. Nobody knows that his present prosperity is founded upon his earlier life as a ruthless and determined bandit. Then a figure from his past arrives in town, threatening to expose his history — and asking Farrance to assist him in securing his lost proceeds from a long-ago train robbery. The colonel acquiesces. But triumph looks to turn to tragedy when Farrance stands to lose all that he holds most precious . . .

MEDICINE FEATHER

Will DuRey

Prospectors in the hills are being ambushed and killed by a gang determined to snatch every ounce of gold that is dug from the ground or panned from the streams. But when one such attack earns the robbers nothing but a pack of pelts, it sets in motion a chain of events leading to a bloody conclusion. For the victim — Medicine Feather, brother of the Arapaho and friend of the Sioux — is unwilling to relinquish his possessions without seeking revenge . . .